To Lu

Thank you ;
to listen to me !!)
doubt I would have
finished writing this if wt for
you. Your creative mind is
so well attuned and I needed
that creative push!!

I hope you enjoy finding
all the grammatical errors
in here!

Love Yasmin :)

ABOUT THE AUTHOR

Yasmin Chloe is has published two pieces of historical fiction, Ezekiel Washed Ashore is her second piece. The novella, The Summers of Arthur Landstone was her first published work.

The author is both a third year history student and an avid fan of early modern history.

Other works by the author:

Fiction

As Yasmin C. Abbas:

The Summers of Arthur Landstone

Non-Fiction

As Yasmin Abbas:

A short introduction to Black Internationalism

Ezekiel

Washed

Ashore

Yasmin Chloe

For my mum Kathleen, who without your constant support I would not have finished...probably ever.

Contents:

PART I – FLOTSAM

PART II – ANCHOR

PART III – DEAD RECKONING

PART I- FLOTSAM

Chapter 1

Surf

I woke up on my desk. I had fallen asleep last night in the middle of reading an old poorly bound paperback about something or other, I forget what exactly. The storm that had blown in that evening was frightful but also so queerly calming that I couldn't help but be carried off into slumber while the tempest raged on just outside my windows.

I had left the candle burning also which was careless and wasteful of me, it made me aware of how much more frugal I had to be with my lamps and candles than ever before, as I had a lot less money than before.

The house felt darker than usual this morning. The morning after a storm is usually so refreshing here, but this morning it is drab. As I am sat in front of the window at my desk I can tell you that there is a good reason; the sky is terribly overcast and the water is the same raw grey-blue. It is calm though. A vast difference from the light before. I can not take the boat out today though, maybe tomorrow.

It's still too soon for me after… Well you know and my shoulder is still not in the best of conditions to work as it is. I can live another few weeks on what I have at home I made a good deal on oysters last market day anyway. Most days I found to be rather low on appetite as it is. Apologies for not writing in so long I have found myself rather preoccupied I am sure looking through my accounts book but is here next to me but for the life of me I can not remember the past few days very well as you can imagine, perhaps I'll lay off the whiskey a little I must accept the reality of what it is eventually. The yard could do with the sorting after the storm and I must check the boat as well.

A most interesting morning I had! I have heard of storms washing up odd items and even the corpses of some wretched souls, but never a living man and child!

I was out sorting the pieces of usual driftwood and flotsam from the storm, when proceeding to my boat there lay a body washed ashore. It most frightened me as you can imagine. I dare say I am lucky to not have had another episode of remembering that horrendous day just by beholding him. As I mentioned, on the shore a little ways down from the boat was a body. I approached it not really expecting the fellow to live. He was terribly tangled with pieces of sea fauna wrapped around his limbs and his clothes were buffeted by the sea to near tatters. I noticed immediately that he was laying face up. And that he was facing the sun, that as usual, was laying behind those ever present clouds. A remarkably handsome face he had to.

His skin was a pallid grey-brown, and almost devoid of life entirely, per my initial thinking that the fellow was dead. It was only when I neared closer to what I believed to be a corpse, that what I at first beheld the piece of sodden wooden board, to which a small bundle of rags was lashed to the man's right arm, with a thick heavy corded rope. In fact it was lashed so tightly that his forearm was bleeding profusely and had the thick cording had dug deeply into his flesh, causing a thick gash to have formed, though the long exposure to the salt water had left the wound with a lurid white grey edge, the flesh of which was dead and bloodless and sagging. The bundle of rags though were not rags at all but a young child; a baby. The plank had been used as a raft to which the small child was held fast to the man's arm and awake no less! It looked to be a little girl from the face, perhaps two years old but small perhaps, it was hard to tell, bundled though she was in a thoroughly sodden rough canvas swaddle.

The child was clearly the man's daughter, the likeness was immediately obvious, but her silence unnerved me slightly. The little girl was making not a sound as she lay tied to the wet decrepit board with her unconscious father laying dying right beside her. She was silently and calmly staring up at those low-hanging grey clouds. I confess, if it were not for the repetitive kicking off her legs in that swaddle, I should have thought the poor child dead. I must admit that for rather a long time I simply stood dumbfounded at what the storm had deposited upon my shore. A child tied to a wooden plank and her dying father, not a native of these shores but somehow so fitting to the scenery with the tranquil expression on his face.

Eventually though I did spur myself into action. I reached first for the child to check that she was well as could be, considering the circumstances, and untied her from the makeshift raft to attend to her father. To my ministrations she made no fuss at all until I placed her, canvas swaddling and all, onto the beach just out of reach of the man. At this she began to fuss and wriggle in that fitful way that babies do. I tried to shush and calm her as best as I could but her agitation only increased. Ideally, I should have gone for help, but with the village was 20 minutes ride on horseback and no horse I had. And overall I feared to leave the child alone should she expire in my absence. So I ignored her cries momentarily to tend to her father.

He was chilled quite thoroughly when I reached to undo the rope that had lashed the board his wounded arm. I noticed that the rope that had been wound so tightly around his forearm had deeply serrated the skin, but tied to this also was a saltwater stained, once golden but now bronze-green linked chain, to which was attached a small oval locket.

I had no time to examine this in detail, for as I was leaning over the fellow I noticed that quiet, harsh gasps were leaving him. The man was like his daughter, and by some miracle alive! I quickly put my ear to his chest and listened and waited. I don't know if it was because I was so expectant, but it felt like too long before I heard the stilted and intermittent beat of his heart. The sound filled me with indescribable joy. It sounded as though he had perhaps unconsciously coughed up any water before I had discovered them, as from what I could hear from his breaths, his lungs did not sound as though they were full of water. However, my happiness at the man's miraculous survival was short lived, as I now had to find a way to get both he and his fussing infant off of the damp and sodden shore and inside where it was dry.

Though my house was not a long way off from the shoreline that bordered it, it would be a tedious trek to haul an unconscious body and the little girl in one trip, and I still had to find them medical attention. I knew of a doctor on the island that I had spoken to only briefly since moving here the past year, but I would need to leave them to get to him, and this new conundrum left me feeling overwhelmed - before the child's cries shook me out of my reverie and I was spurred once again into action to save the lives of these two washed up guests.

I decided, and you may think me wrong to have done this, to moved the man first. He seemed to be in a worse condition than the child, who I believed would not expire. I had the choice of dragging the poor man the few yards to my home or carrying him. In the end I decided to carry him as he appeared only slight, with long lean limbs that I figured would not be excessively heavy. However, there was still the problem of my shoulder to contend with. After the accident I was having enough trouble pulling in nets, never mind a fully grown man. I decided therefore to carry him on my back as I sometimes carry the full nets.

He was horribly wet, and I pulled his soaking and wounded arm around my neck and across my shoulder, as I felt the salty cold water seep into the back of my cardigan. His wound began to bleed again at the new jostling and started to seep down my right shoulder in a lurid dark patch, it being expanded by the sea water still clinging to him. It dripped thickly across my chest, as I hoisted the rest of his slight form up onto my back further. His long legs, covered only in tatters hung limply against the back of my own, and banged against the backs of my knees with each step.

With him sufficiently deposited against my back, his unconscious head lolling heavily against my left shoulder; for the third time that morning paused. And embarrassed as I am to admit it; laughed. The situation was simply too absurd for me to take it much seriously, I believe I was likely in shock. There I stood on the shore with an unconscious man hanging against my back straining my sore shoulder, with an infant at my feet staring at me curiously. And curious I did look. The hilarity or perhaps the shock of the situation being so bizarre but yet so severe, forced the laugh out of me in a startling an unseemly hiccup, to the point that I almost pitched forward with my morose bundle. And it took me a moment to begin walking up the beach proper, with the man hoisted against me.

Through habit, that I haven't changed since living on so remote an island, I had neglected to lock the door earlier that morning and simply had to free a single arm to turn the handle. Once inside, I concluded that the most spacious place to deposit the man was the sitting room, the lounge not being large enough and wanting for chairs. The sitting room however, had ample space to leave the unconscious body.

I wasted little time, as I left him with his head propped against the armrest of the divan, before I headed outside to retrieve the girl. She had not moved from where I had placed her before I moved her father, and lay there on her back mutely staring at the never changing clouds that constantly paraded in the bleak sky above her. Moving her was no contest; she made no fuss and as I placed her in my arms I marvelled at how she had weathered the storm, and presumably some wreck, better than her father; and at such a young age no less! I hesitated to say so earlier should you think badly of me, but I felt a small spark pang of jealousy at this man for having a daughter that was alive and seemingly well, for my child had perished.

I will not dwell on that. These thoughts are intrusive and rather negative.

I preceded to quickly survey the surf as far out as I could from where I stood on the beach for any other washed up bodies. It surprised me that I hadn't even thought to look prior, but I put that down to being relatively distracted by these two castaways. The search thankfully was fruitless and there were no other bodies to be seen for as far as I could ascertain. Satisfied with my observation, I made my way up the beach back home.

I had left the door unlocked on my way out but holding the small girl in the crook of my good arm, I had no concerns of whether or not I would be able to carry her and open the door simultaneously. Immediately upon entering the sitting room, I saw that the man lay exactly where I had left him moments ago and had not awoke, which was both concerning but also a relief. It was not through wishing him to not awake, but that I was not entirely sure what I was to do now that I had brought them both inside.

For a beat I merely stood dumbly at the threshold of the sitting room, with the young child in my arms. The room that I was used to seeing empty everyday, seemed foreign to me as I stood there. The awful peeling coral-tone wallpaper seemed as though it belonged to another home that was not mine. And the stranger I had laying on my settee only added to my thoughts of not belonging. I could not help but feel like an intruder in my own home. A most bizarre feeling. Even the photographs that flanked the timepiece above the mantel looked slightly out of place to me. One of the frames I noticed was slightly cracked along the bottom, something that I had never noticed before. It was while I stood there numbly, staring at the picture-frame of all things, that the man shifted. I'm not even sure if he truly did or if I imagined it, but it felt like the air around the room changed faintly, and it was that that alerted me to his awakening. I hadn't even done anything to aid him, but he was coming around on his own. I think it was probably an imperceptible shift of his head that alerted me to his consciousness. I found myself moving forward almost automatically to aid him, the child still secure in my arms.

I moved to kneel close to his head, the child firmly clasped in my arms, as we both tentatively beheld the sluggish movements of the man. I believe I called out to him, though I forget exactly what I said to him now. Most likely casual phrases to try and raise the man's attention. It did not have the desired effect however, and the man merely moved his head again, though this time slightly slower almost though he was responding to something in his sleep. But other than a noticeable increase in the depth of his breathing, he stayed entirely unconscious. I felt there was not much more I could do to raise him, and believed it better to allow him to wake on his own. However, his shifting around had made me catch sight of his arm that was now bleeding into the embroidery of my settee.

Getting up with the baby still clasped in my left arm, I headed into the kitchen where I kept some first aid instruments that someone, I forget who, gifted me on my moving here last year. I brought a towel I kept in there to the sitting room also, the stain would never leave the couch but I could perhaps dab away some of the deep staining.

Upon returning to the room the man was just as I had expected, he had not arose and was still laying with his head cocked to the side, looking for all the world as though he was simply sleeping if not for the bloody gash that was seeping into the worn upholstery. I noticed also that his skin was filling again with colour, the grey-brown hue that he had worn when he was on the shore was mostly gone, and his skin had now filled out into a fairly even light-brown tone a shade or two lighter than my own. His breathing, I noticed was also vastly deeper than it had been previously, and he was mostly breathing through his mouth which I took as a good sign of not having obstructed lungs.

I knew I would have to place the child down to attend to the father but was unsure if she would again, like when I removed her from the board, kick up a fuss. I looked into her face for a moment, and her small face looked back with her cold black eyes fairly unblinking. Frivolously I wondered if her father had the same deep black eyes as his daughter, whose deaths held me momentarily before I strode towards the division and placed her down as gently as I could. Her garments were intact and unlike her father's; the canvas she was wrapped in likely due to that, but nevertheless just as sodden. I watched for a moment as the heavy fabric deposited great spreading swathes of water into the divan's cushions. As she seemed fairly at peace, and not as uncomfortable as she must have been in those wet clothes, I attended to her father.

The wound upon his arm had seeped awfully into the settee and I had half a mind to put the entire piece of furniture down to be unsalvageable. Reaching his arm was rather finicky, as I must admit that I was rather careless in my depositing of him onto the couch. I had to roll him bodily towards me and propped his torso against extra cushions to get his arm into a reachable position to work on. I had next to no issues with bandaging his arm. Though he was slightly damp, the time in which he had been laying there was sufficient to shirk the majority of seawater clinging to him onto the upholstery. This close up I noticed that his clothes were mostly tattered, and the arm that was wounded was basically devoid of a sleeve up to his shoulder. At this close perspective, and with less of the initial shock, I couldn't help but notice his features. They were vastly different from my own broad and stocky frame.

The man was fairly slender but fairly tall and willowy. His svelte limbs looked fairly delicate, and I wondered how he had managed to keep that board lashed to his arm without it damaging it further. His arms for instance were fairly thin and devoid of any muscle that I could see and sparsely covered with hair, the same I assumed for his legs. He was missing a boot, and his feet were rather dainty I thought at a glance. I fleetingly wondered if it was easier or harder to get well-fitting boots with such slender arches. The thought passed quickly from my mind and I instead turned my attention to the man's face. He had shifted since his initial false-awakening, and his eyelashes still held crystalline droplets of water along the very tips. As I remarked previously, the washed out grey hue was slowly leaving him and his face had now taken on a pleasant light brown but for his lips. He had a fairly large forehead and close cropped hair that had coiled tighter with being so sodden with water as it was.

Bandaging his arm as well as I could, I left the man to rest, releasing those even deep breaths as he now was, and turned my attention back to the child. The entire time I had been working on her father she had made no noise, not even while staring at the copious amounts of blood that had stained the cushions, slowly dampening the furniture she was placed on as she watched. I forget where I placed the sodden cloth and bandages before I went to her, but the thought to wrapping something dry around her came to me rather belatedly, as I left her in the room with her unconscious father to seek out the age softened woollen blanket I kept on the wooden seat by the door. Upon my return she had not moved and I believed had been silently taking in the countenance of her father until I arrived untimely back into the room and interrupted her infantile staring. Upon my approach her large eyes fixed themselves firstly onto my face and then onto the blanket I was holding, the glance was fairly fleeting and she made a quiet gurgle as though in consent to being swaddled.

I wasted no time in stepping towards her and wrapping her small limbs into the warm fabric. It was at this time that I had decided the best following course of action would be to take her to Doctor Potter. Having no telephone, like many of the islanders I would have to surprise the old man at his home. I figured that the man would be unlikely to me to wake before I could get to the Doctor's house and back, and decided to leave a note explaining where I had gone, where his daughter was and in fact where he himself was; as he was unlikely to know upon waking in my absence. I left the note by the divan that sat across from the settee in which he slept and hoped that the stark white of the stationary would stand out well enough against the dark mauve of the seat cushion. With the note in place and the baby in my arms I stepped out, leaving the front door unlocked but closed should the man awake and feel in anyway trapped.

The day was as still as ever. The water was eerily calm as it always was just before noon but seemed all the more strange in contrast to the bulging swells and waves of the night before. The beach front was mostly empty from my earlier clearing and the grey of the shale and sand, merged with the washed out blue of the surf, only to be blended into the empty grey-white sky; forming a never-ending expanse of grey landscape.

The interior of the island was not much more joyful. My home is isolated. It is cut off from the denser village by a large grove or more likely small wood of trees, I believe this is where the island gets its name. Grove island is named just so, simply because of that very same grove I live next to. Around the area is only one more house but Mrs. Smith, from the village, has told me that it was abandoned since she was a child. Though it is clearly very old, it is not dilapidated and I sometimes pretend I have a close neighbour. The majority of houses on the island were closer together but not in the same way they are in cities. Each house or cottage is usually fairly far off from a neighbour, though occasionally there are one or two that are situated on the same land. Doctor Potter was conveniently my closest neighbour. He and his wife Delilah had been on the island before I, and had welcomed me extremely warmly when I first arrived. Despite being my neighbour though, the Potters lived a good 20 minutes walk away from my home, perched on a slight incline just past the grove but closer to the village than myself.

The walk there was the same as I have always remembered it to be. Though bare of most plant life, burrowing into the grove, and creeping out onto the main footpath were ceaseless tendrils of small vines and shallow squat bushes. The path was the only one on the island. It wound around and through the whole island like a dusty, gravelled serpent and connected all homes and conveniences on one long solemn road of rock and dust. The haphazard topography of the island made seeing far off tricky at times, and places in the distance would at one moment be in sight and clear, and the next be obstructed by a hillock or large boulder.

The Potters cottage was quaint, and fit naturally into the calm quiet mood of the island, and despite its modern panelling, looked almost as though it had been stood there since the island itself was formed. Drastically dissimilar to my peeling and ever-creaking two storey shore-front house, the Potters cottage was a simple single storey, thatched roof abode that looked like an idyllic home that had been pulled directly out of a child's storybook. It was also the only house that I knew of on the island with such a plenitude of flowers, that grew in a spectrum of colours, which was bizarre, as all of the flowers that were known to grow on Grove Island were a stark, sickly white, and shaped like large, colourless forget-me-nots. The front windows similarly were lined with dainty window-boxes that contained variations of colourful flowers, with plentiful vibrant green leaves protruding from the stems. I couldn't tell you what flowers they were as I'm terrible at that sort of thing, and every time I ask Delilah she responds with a different answers to their breed. I have a suspicion that she doesn't know their breeds either, and have stopped asking. The gravel path connected the Potters house just as it did all the houses on the island, but the gravel changed to soft sand and became interwoven with grass instead of hard shale on the way up.

The grove flanks the left of the path that leads to the Potters cottage, and I have a habit of peering through that dense treeline whenever I walk along the path. If you were to turn back to face the opposite way and look in the right place, it's possible to see a minute speck of dirty-white *something*, that breaks up the dense collection of tree tones – it's my home.

And it looks so lonely and small from the other side of the Grove.

I did not get far along the path past the thickness of the grove, perhaps about halfway, before the door opened and out stepped Mrs Potter. She was a round squat woman, who had a head of perfectly silver hair that she kept pinned up around her head like a grey halo. I had been told by Mr Potter, in a conversation I forget the origin of now, that Delilah's hair reached down to her waist, and I always wondered how many hairpins it took for her to pin her hair up as she did.

As I walked up their path carrying the little girl in my arms I could see, but not quite hear her calling out some form of greeting to me from her doorway, and then saw her turn her head behind her to call into the house likely for Graham. By the time I had reached the front door, Graham Potter was already there peering out behind his wife who was calling out to me as I approached nearer, the delighted look on their elderly faces changed to curiosity at the bundle I held in my arms. It was as I got within a few paces of the doorway and the child began to shuffle around in my arms that spurred Delilah to reach out toward me. The trade off with the baby was not unexpected and I followed Delilah into the house as she cooed and talked in that way that people do when in the presence of infants.

Once inside and I had to briefly explained the situation to the retired doctor, he wasted no time in checking her over. Though only a single storey, the Potters home was in similar layout to the front of my own downstairs floor, and with the sitting room being placed in the same area as my own, the home always felt very familiar to me. One stark contrast however, was the increased light that the Potters sitting room was blessed with. Unlike my drab and grey-washed interior, the Potters home had a bright and warm glow to the rooms that felt well lived in and comforting.

I sat across from Doctor Potter as he lay the child on the cushion beside him on the couch and watched him examine her. I don't know how long I sat there but it couldn't have been that long as, Mrs Potter soon reappeared from her earlier disappearance, bearing a bundle of cloths and needle-worked fabric what I took to be items for the child. It was only once the good doctor had finished his exam and Mrs Potter had changed her out of the old, dirty clothes, after berating me for keeping her in them, that the doctor suggested we returned to my home immediately to look upon the unconscious man. I agreed and with the little girl newly swaddled, with promises from Mrs Potter to have some baby clothes by the end of the day, myself and Graham ladened with his medical equipment, left to see to the man.

•••

I was once again, sat across from the Doctor watching him work, this time however it was not a child he was working on but a man. A fully conscious man, who was sat upright staring at me as I held his child in my arms.

As we had arrived the man had not left as I had suspected he might do if he were to wake, but had been sitting up on the blood soaked settee with his feet planted on the rug and his head resting in his hands. The noise of the door and the happy gurgle from the child caused him to snap his head up at our party entry, his face was drawn and haggard and. much different from his sleeping face. However, this was not entirely surprising, seeing as he had woken up in a strange house with his daughter nowhere in sight; the situation would

36

have worried anyone. What was surprising though, were the man's eyes. I had taken the deep sinking brown of little girls as being the same as those of her father, and they clearly were. But only the left one. The man's right eye was thickly clouded with white film; a blind eye, but nonetheless intrinsically beautiful as the first.

On our entry into the doorway the man's eyes alighted on the doctor's bespectacled face behind me, then to my own face which I don't doubt was wearing a deeply surprised expression, and then to the little girl who was tucked carefully into the cradle of my arms. Upon seeing his daughter the man stood hastily and stretched out his arms still clad in tatters towards her. However, I know not if from blood loss or prolonged unconsciousness, the man immediately pitched forward into a swoon and if it were not for the doctor's quick movements, would likely have fallen entirely and dashed his head against the side of the table that he was a hairsbreadth away from collapsing into. I had of course instinctively stepped forward to help the man but would have been unable to sufficiently help carrying the child as I was, and so instead placed myself down on the divan across from the settee in which the doctor was coaxing the man back onto to begin his examination.

It was then how I found myself under the scrutiny of this man as he stared at me in an unexplainable way, occasionally switching his focus to his happily gurgling and squirming daughter who rested in my lap all the while absently answering whichever questions the doctor posed.

It so happened that just as supposed, the two were castaways from a wreck the night of the big storm. They were travelling from the Americas on their way to England to live with relatives. The man, Ezekiel Forge was a clerk who was taking his daughter Sarah to live with his sister in London, where he had been offered a job, he said, in publishing house and was to start within the month. With a laugh he supposed that would no longer be the case. The man spoke with an American lilt that was speckled with various twanging vowels that sounded Portuguese or maybe Spanish. Nevertheless, his accent was strong but also rather peaceable. It was due to this that his outward and unceasing staring began to bother me less and as I listened to him speaking about his life in America, I think he said Carolina or maybe Kansas, I found my attention straying to look around the room. I almost never sat in the sitting room as it's too cold usually, but with four people in it it, it wasn't so bad, and made me wonder what it would have been like had Esther and the child had survived.

I was broken out of this sombre reverie by the child, who had shifted to no longer trying to make prolonged eye contact with her father, to looking up at me. It was only then that I notice the room was no longer held the deep smooth tones of the doctor's voice, nor Ezekiel's soft responses. When I looked up I noticed that the doctor was also looking at me expectantly as waiting for something. I apologised for my inattention to which he pardoned, but repeated that despite his ordeal the man was in relatively good health with no sign of fever or infection in the wound on his arm, and whether or not I had any spare clothes I might lend him. I cursed myself for not thinking of preparing a change of clothes beforehand and agreeing that I did, quickly and awkwardly placed the child in the outstretched and waiting hands of her father, and left the room to find some suitable clothes. I knew at a glance that I was of a stockier build than the man, though he was much taller and leaner than I. Despite this I knew I had some clothes that would fit somewhat comfortably on him, for now.

The scene upon my return to the sitting room was warming. The drab and cold light of the sitting room seemed to be washed away with the figures that occupied it. The man sat more fully upright with his daughter in his lap who was being entertained by the doctor's stethoscope, the image was so comforting that I couldn't help but feel as though I was destroying the moment by announcing my arrival as I did. The joyous expression on the man's face however,, did not change. When placing his daughter into the arms of the doctor, he stepped up to me and taking my hand in his thanked me rather profusely for saving his life and the life of his little girl. I told him it was what anyone would do but he would not hear of it, claiming he would repay me in anyway he was able. I told him there was no need of course, and that he and Sarah may stay as long as they needed to recover before leaving for London. This offer I thought to be rather basic, but the man seemed close to tears when he thanked me again and rather unnecessarily, I thought, drew me into a great big hug while thanking me for my kindness. The shock must have shown openly on my face, for Sarah began to giggle for all she was worth. This in turn made the doctor smile and releasing me from his hug, Ezekiel himself was smiling rather broadly. I found the entire confrontation so bizarre that I in turn let out a short laugh of happiness too.

Ezekiel stood back and still clasping onto my shoulders for a moment before dropping his hands and reaching for the bundle of clothes I held in my own arms. I pass them over to him rather dimly. And without much ceremony. he stepped past me into the corridor and for a moment turned his head in question. I merely pointed up the stairs and replied to his unspoken question that he may use any of the rooms to change, all the doors were unlocked. With a swift nod and that pleasant smile back on his face, Ezekiel barefoot, trotted quickly up the steps in his tattered clothes, his lone boot had been removed earlier during in the doctors examination. Watching Ezekiel's bare feet disappear up the stairs reminded me to find a spare pair of boots I kept in the entryway trunk. My feet I knew were much larger than his but I figured he might place some cloth in them to fill them. They would do until he might make his way to London. I wasn't sure what the procedures for shipwrecks and salvage were, but I assumed that there might be some authority that could be contacted to ascertain whether anything from the ship had been found.

I forget what the doctor and I spoke about while we waited for Ezekiel to return from changing. I do remember that the child had fallen asleep, this surprised me as up until this point she had remained completely awake. She seemed comfortable enough in Doctor Potters arms though, and so I did not bother to suggest setting a place for her to rest.

Ezekiel's re-emergence was markedly less dramatic to his leaving. I offered the boots to him which he politely accepted, giving me time to notice that the clothes, as I anticipated, were far too big for him. The bottoms came well above his ankles and almost to his mid calf, thankfully the brace I included kept them sufficiently up. The shirt was also comically too large for his slight form and he had rolled the cuffs over the sleeve of the knitwear I provided to keep them out of the way. The only garment that did fit somewhat better was the cardigan that Ren had made for me when I moved first came to the island, and was a perfect fit for him.

Upon Ezekiel's return Sarah had not awoken, but had shifted in Dr Potters arms, the movement pulled Ezekiel's intense look from myself to his daughter, whom in a couple of strides had cradled in his arms. The doctor satisfied with the health of both Ezekiel and Sarah claimed he would check on them both tomorrow and bring some suitable clothing for Sarah that Delilah was fashioning at this very moment. Amidst his leisurely packing away of his instruments, Graham remarked on the absence of Sarah's mother and expressed his concern that she had not been lost in the wreck. The question was an obvious one, but it had not occurred to me to have asked it prior. The question seemed almost to take

Ezekiel off guard, who was at that moment stood holding Sarah and looking into her quiet sleeping face. The question had him halt in his gentle swaying and look to the doctor and then away again, past where he was sat on the settee and out the large sitting room window that looked out onto the beach front. There was a beat of silence before the doctor apologised for the intrusive question and that he meant no offence by it. Ezekiel did not respond for a while but after a short pause he appeared to flick out of his sombre thoughts and turned his attention to the doctor, smiling as claimed no offence had been taken and that his wife and Sarah's mother had left soon after giving birth to Sarah. With a bitter smile Ezekiel added after a moment that he believed his wife wished for a more interesting life than he could provide, at this last comment he looked down at Sarah still wearing that pleased smile of his, firmly fixed upon his face, and I wondered fleetingly if it was at all strained.

By that time the shadows in the sitting room had begun to lengthen and the generic pale-blue light was slowly diminishing to a murky grey-blue as the evening approached. The stillness of the water felt more oppressive and the noiselessness of the island more apparent. With the fading light, the doctor took his leave, stepping onto the front porch step to turn back to Ezekiel once more, who stood a foot or so behind me in the doorway clasping Sarah to his chest. The doctor repeated his earlier promise of checking in tomorrow, and hoisted his bag as he meandered down off the step and made his careful way along the beach to his own home in the pale twilight, his old form slowly ambling along. Ezekiel and I stood shoulder to shoulder now in the open doorway watching the form of Doctor Potter disappear past the grove, that in the low-light looked more expensive than it truly was, it seemed to swallow up all the light that may have been able to permeate through it. As usual the sky was blanketed by cloud and barring the way to any moonlight that may have made a difference to the oncoming night.

Once the form of doctor Potter had entirely disappeared, I turned away to face Ezekiel, and was about to ask him if he was hungry before he spoke, still staring out into the twilight. At the time I did not think much of my response, but now I wonder why it did not seem strange to me. He asked if the sky was always that colour. I was of course slightly taken aback by the question, as I had been thinking of supper not the sky. But I believe I responded by replying that yes the sky was always rather cloudy with snippets of sunshine every once in awhile. The island was prone to rain, I explained and the altitude of it made it seem always as though it was dusk or dawn, as it never really got fully dark for long. I had read that in a book somewhere, and relayed all of this to Ezekiel. My response seemed to satisfy him as he nodded his head once, still looking out into the fading light, stating that it was unusual, but he could get used to the feeling. I thought that a rather odd thing to say, but thought no more of it. It was now that I made my offer of supper to him, which pulled him out of his musings and that beatific smile returned, as he exclaimed that he was famished having not eaten since he boarded the ship. I forewarned him that the repassed would not be a feast, as I had only some fish and some bread. In response Ezekiel, whose smile had broadened, now resettled

Sarah in his arms and began to make his way to the kitchen calling back to me that fish was the only thing he knew how to make. As he disappeared around the kitchen door jab I notice rather belatedly, that he was unabashedly barefoot.

•••••

It was well into the night before we three sat down to my meagre offering of dinner. Though Sarah was still fast asleep, there was a slowly cooling mug of goat's milk placed in front of Ezekiel, waiting for her when she awoke from her sleep in the crook of Ezekiel's unwounded arm. The other arm, though bandaged tightly, Ezekiel was using to feed himself seemingly unconcerned with the wound. In-between large bites of fried fish and sparsely buttered bread Ezekiel told me of his life before he left America. He had been a happily married man and clerk in North Carolina, before his wife Ruth declared that the entire family should seek out a new life in Haiti as her cousin Frederick (I think he said he had been called) had done a year earlier and was living a much freer and beautiful life. The idea seemed reckless to Ezekiel as they had just had Sarah, and the

47

move seemed unnecessary as he made more than enough money to support them. Overtime it so happened that Ruth felt that she needed to leave alone and so did, in the dead of night no less. Leaving Ezekiel and their barely a year old daughter to start a new life in a country she only knew about from her cousin's letters. It turns out that shortly after this Ezekiel had thought it better for Sarah growing up if they were to relocate to London where Ezekiel's elder sister would be able to look after Sarah along with her own children, and Ezekiel could find new employment also. The disaster with the ship had however, entirely derailed his plans. At this point Ezekiel had finished eating with his sole hand and looked up at me smiling that same pleasant smile of his, as he remarked that I knew the rest of the story to date, and once again thanked me for taking him in. I assured him that it was of no consequence and that I was glad of the company. Although I hesitated initially, I did ask him how long he wished to stay on the island. I did not want it to sound as though I wished him gone however, and tried to keep my tone as pleasant and conversational as possible. The question seemed to catch Ezekiel off guard despite my efforts, and although his smile remained firmly fixed on his face, his eyes flickered away from mine and moved down to the face of his quietly sleeping child. There was no response from him for quite some time, so long in fact that I was unsure whether he had heard the question at all, and I cleared my throat to repeat it before he spoke. The tone with which he responded was wistful and almost sad. He said that the past day here had made him question whether or not he should be heading for London straight away. He said he felt like he *belonged* on the island, and wasn't sure if it wasn't by some divine providence that he arrived here. The last sentence seemed to be a thought that he meant not to share and he laughed at the severity that had been in his tone with the quip that he must have washed ashore this particular island for some reason. It was then that his smile brightened and the light in his eyes increased with genuine mirth. This brief spout of merriment was cut short by a stifled yawn that made me realise that I too was rather more tired than I had at first realised, and that Ezekiel must be far more tired than I. I suggested that it would be a convenient time for me to show him the spare room, as we had both by this time finished our food and Sarah had not awoke for her milk. Ezekiel agreed and standing fluidly with Sarah secure in his arms, I motioned him to lead the way out of the dim kitchen into the darkened corridor.

The house by this time was swallowed by the pitch of night and it was necessary to light a small withered candle that I kept in the kitchen to light the way up the stairs and to the room. I had not prepared this room per say, it had come fully furnished like rest the rest of the house; filled with a large wrought iron bed, an imposing chest of drawers and an enormous antique bronze mirror that faced the bed at an odd angle. The room was next to my own and was deeply spacious, with two sets of alcove windows that stood parallel to the door and exactly as the ones in my bedroom, stood to have a perfect view of the beach-front. Unfortunately due to the entirely overcast night they gave out no bright illumination, except that eerie light that comes with the nighttime on the island- a night that is never fully dark and bathes the atmosphere in a deep, dreary, old grey-blue hue. I explained to Ezekiel that the bathroom was the door across from him the room in which we stood, and bade him goodnight, to which he returned heartily as I closed the door behind myself.

I stood in the corridor a moment and took a minute to breathe. It was a strange feeling having a stranger in my home. Having lived on this island for the past year and after Esther, I had forgotten what it felt like to have other people so close. I rarely spoke to doctor Potter or Delilah despite them being my closest neighbours. As I stood there, I listened to the sounds of Ezekiel making ready for bed and that oddly accented voice murmuring I supposed to Sarah. I did not hear her though and took her to be still be asleep. I had not realised I was stood so taunt listening until all sounds from the room stopped and I understood Ezekiel to fully settled down to sleep. It was only then that I moved away to my own room, avoiding the spattering of loose floorboard as I went.

That night I prepared slowly for sleep. I anticipated a night of wakefulness due to such an eventful day and felt no immediate wish to get under the covers and wait for dawn as my insomnia-riddled mind had forced me to do so many nights before. As I was placing my boots under my bed, as I do every night, the thought struck me that Ezekiel had still been barefoot up to my leaving him in the room next door. The thought made me smile and still in just my shirt and trousers I made my way, clad in just my own socks, down the stairs to the sitting room where just as I had left them hours before, the boots I had fetched for Ezekiel stood waiting for me. I don't know what it was exactly that made me go down there and check. Perhaps curiosity.

I carried them back up to Ezekiel's door and though the thought crossed my mind to knock, I remembered Sarah was asleep and simply placed the boots outside the door but out of the way so Ezekiel would see them in the coming morning but not trip over them. Feeling that I had accomplished something, I made my way back to my room only glancing briefly at that photo that stood resolute upon my nightstand, as I settled myself under the covers.

I did not attempt to feign sleep as I had so many nights before, neither did I try to read the novel I had on my my side table, that had remained unopened for the past week. This was rather unlike me, as I tended to enjoy reading when I had the time, however I felt no inclination to that night, my mind instead was filled with the events of the day and replaying every moment of it.

Since moving to the island, my days had been fairly mundane and the excitement of today was startling to say the least. That night I stared into the ever encroaching shadows of my room in the dusky darkness, and to my genuine surprise I slept that night. I don't know how long it took me to fall asleep as you never really do know, but I remember beginning to feel tired. What was truly astonishing about that night thought, was just before I slept I was staring absently out the large windows whose curtains I always keep open to let in the dusky, dim light of the cloud-banked sky. That night the usual dense blanket of clouds that haunted the sky was peaceably fragmented by a small tear in the clouds, that gave way to a delicate patch of inky black. Revealed along with it was a lone, but immensely bright star that shone ethereally out from the blackness. The sight was so rare, I remember wondering if I was dreaming. For as far as I could recall, I had not yet seen a star in the night sky of this island for all my time living there. The star was the last thing I remember before succumbing to sleep. I stared at it intently, fearing if I looked away or even blinked it would again be swallowed up by the dense clouds.

Chapter 2
Dampen

The morning felt remarkably different. I had startled myself awake almost, with the surprise at having fallen asleep at all, and the bright greyish-white dawn that washed through my windows was an unexpected sensation. Usually I wake slowly and peaceably, if I had fallen asleep at all, but that morning I felt as though I had been entirely dragged from my slumber and forcibly shaken awake by invisible hands. What added to the unusual feeling of that morning was the hyper-aware sense that I was not in fact alone in my house. Not that I could particularly hear them next door, despite the walls being extraordinarily thin, but I was aware nonetheless of their presence and that was jarring enough. I took my time getting up that morning, and for a long time I simply lay tucked under the lightly starched covers just taking in the feeling of early morning. I had no watch or clock, for I never really felt the need for one and had become excellent at gauging the time of day by the dismal light, and through this simple means I took it then to be around 6:00 or 7:00 o'clock in the morning long past low tide. The gentle wash of the surf against the shore could be heard from almost all parts of the house and the morning was as it always had been since they had gone.

I listened to the waves so gentle now, and so unlike *that* day. Though I tried to prevent my thoughts from turning negative so early, I couldn't help but turn my head to glance at my nightstand. The photo had stood there since the accident. It was a half-body photograph of Esther and her bump was just visible at the bottom of the frame; I stared at that photograph for quite some time before I moved my gaze back to the window. A large set of wings swung by and I knew that it would not be long before the gulls began screeching their incessant early morning call.

I heaved myself out of the comfort of my bed and made ready for the day, more sedate than I care to admit. The momentary melancholy that came with remembering Esther so bitterly, had soured my mood and I attempted to take the time to calm myself before I ventured out and greeted Ezekiel and little Sarah. The thought of the two of them improved my dower feeling, and by the time I slipped my feet into yesterday's socks I was much more improved in spirit.

Before making my way downstairs I stopped just before leaving my room, my hand firmly wrapped around the doorknob but not yet turning it. I considered if it better to wake Ezekiel before making a start on breakfast; which would be the tantalising repast of oats and weak coffee again. As the previous night, I hovered uncertainly at the door and took a moment to listen, should I hear any noise in the room. Hearing nothing after a minute or so, I decided that I would make breakfast anyway and call up after it was all set. I had never been host to anyone before, not since moving to the island and the feeling was odd but rather comforting; knowing that I would be looking after somebody else.

I fear I am fixating on the accident far too much, as it is still fresh in my mind. I know they say you should never forget the people that you have lost, but I feel as though I worry too much about what *could* have happened.

Midway through boiling oats in a large dented pot, the soft tread of Ezekiel's still un-booted feet could be heard making their way down the stairs in a careful and sedate pace that suggested he was carrying Sarah. And not long after a hearty *good morning* was announced from the doorway, supplied by a gleeful babble from Sarah. The greetings caused me to turn around and match the pleasant smiles directed at me with my own, supplemented with my own return of the greeting though I assume I did not sound as chipper as they did (it was not in my natural inclination to do so). I explained and mildly apologised for the sparse breakfast as Ezekiel made his way further into the kitchen. During which he made his own apologies for being such a late riser and offered to help in some way. Truly there was nothing to be done in regards to preparing the meagre meal but the earnestness and the guilt that decorated Ezekiel's face made me direct him in laying out the cups and bowls on the small table that was chipped and worn-out through years of use. Partially to keep him busy and partially so I could observe him unattended. His demeanour was relatively unchanged since he had awoken yesterday, he had a cheerfulness that belied his wounded arm and horrific encounter of being shipwrecked and almost drowned to death.

The clothes I gave him yesterday still hung on him in a comical oversized fashion and his feet though covered with thick coarse socks that I had lent him were still shoeless and danced around my small kitchenette as free as ever. The urge to ask why he had not put on the boots almost passed my lips once or twice as the bizarreness of seeing those woollen toes peek out from oversized trousers prevented me, and on the third attempt in asking him, I gave up and instead announced that the porridge was ready and if Sarah was old enough to eat any.

The sun had fully risen behind the clouds at this point and the dull bars of light that blandly illuminated the windows, gave the morning inside that kitchen a sad and gaunt pale, grey hue. However, the liveliness of my small kitchen repelled the bleakness of the day. That a morning, in-between feeding Sarah who was propped up on the table resting against a heavy stack of assorted books that I had on the sideboard, Ezekiel conversed gaily as ever with me about a various multitude of topics; many of which I believed he was not at all truly interested in, but as they had entered into his mind, he found worth talking about to me. One of which was the state of his arm. I couldn't see the condition of his injury under the cover of the bandages as he had rolled the sleeves down today; presumably tucked into the cuffs of the jumper, but his freedom of movement I took to be a good sign. He was also using two spoons at once after all, and I assumed then that Ezekiel was either much stronger than he looked or he was bravely ignoring the pain entirely.

When I asked him directly about his wound he laughed deeply and claimed it hurt only a little, and was a trade he was willing to accept in the place of drowning at sea with the possibility of never seeing his daughter again. This last comment sparked a sad look in his eye and seemed also to upset Sarah, who though I was unsure whether or not she understood what had been said, seemed to pick up on the sadness of the tone and began to fuss which turned Ezekiel's attention away from me. Which I was enormously thankful for, as it prevented him from seeing the wince on my face. I could not blame him for the comment as he did not know about Esther, but the shock of the statement caught me thoroughly off guard and I attempted to recentre myself by taking a too long drink of coffee which being still hot, both burnt my tongue and distracted me enough to draw my attention back to Ezekiel, the emotions completely erased from my face.

Sarah seemed settled now and had begun playing with the small gold locket I had seen before wound around Ezekiel's arm. It was just as I was about to make a query of the piece of jewellery that a gentle but firm knock resounded from the front door and echoed through the hallway and into the kitchen. Assuming it was doctor Potter arriving as he said he would, I excused myself and went to answer the door, all thoughts of Esther and drowning pushed firmly to the back of my mind.

It was in fact Graham Potter who stood on my stoop and I let him in without much ceremony. I immediately noticed however, that he was carrying a large canvas wrapped bundle under his arm along with his usual medical bag placed in the other. Following my gaze the doctor assured me that it was just a gift for our "washed-up friend" as he put it, as the crows feet beside his eyes crinkled lovingly as he spoke. Despite the peaceable mirth in his voice the doctor looked somewhat more detached and almost far away. Before I let him into the kitchen I felt the need to ask him if all was well. The question seemed to shake Graham out of his reverie, and he replied in an extremely low and unhappy voice that Delilah had moved on.

This was the second statement that morning to shake me so down to the core and lost for words I merely clutched the doctor's elbow tightly, squeezed once and let go. Graham looked me squarely in the face and nodding his head in thanks hefted the canvas bundle higher under his aged but firm arm and stepped around me, leading the way to the kitchen.

It turned out that before Delilah left, she had sewn a large assortment of babies items including; three soft ivory dresses (that Graham assured me were made out of old pillow cases they no longer needed), two sets of bloomers (made from the same fabric), two bonnets (that were delicately crocheted), as well as a large knitted sea-foam green baby blanket that I couldn't help thinking was the exact colour of the sea that morning. There were also three sets of knitted boots in various shades of brown, as well as a small but warm looking light-blue cardigan which was softer than anything, as I ran my fingers over it. The sheer quality of these many items impressed me and Ezekiel greatly, who made appreciative and grateful comments for every item as he picked them up in turn.

The look of pride in Graham's face was beatific, however this was not all that lay in the canvas wrap. Doctor Potter had also included two spare shirts of his own and a pair of trousers as well as a worn wool jacket, all of which he claimed to be too small for him as he was now a much more 'round around the middle' than he used to be and could no longer fit in them, and that they were Ezekiel's if he wished to have them. Ezekiel's answer to this was to coax old Potter into the chair he had been occupying at the table, and personally pour him a cup of now lukewarm coffee all the while thanking him and Delilah profusely for the items, and making earnest promises to repay him back in the near future for his kindness.

Doctor Potters check-over was efficient and quick as he re-bandaged Ezekiel's wound proficiently, and after checking Sarah over, who giggled and kicked her little legs the entire time before he pronounced her fit and healthy, Doctor Potter drained the last of his coffee and without much fanfare left. As he departed leaving his gifts and goodwill behind, I couldn't help but notice how sad his face appeared. I thought it best to leave him for the moment and check on him again tomorrow, to not overburden him after Delilah's leaving.

••••

By low tide that afternoon Ezekiel and Sarah, who was fully bedecked in bonnet, booties and new dress were sat playing in front of the empty fireplace. Again with the brass-like gold locket. That necklace always seemed to work in distracting Sarah considerably. Unlike before, Ezekiel was not dangling the Locket in front of Sarah, instead he wore it around his neck. The broken clasp forgotten as he tied the delicately linked chain in a small knock to the back of his neck.

At this point in the afternoon when the shadows were not yet long enough to reach over to the centre of the room where we were sat, Ezekiel made a comment that though shook me out of my musing was something was nagging at my subconscious the day before. Ezekiel however, with Sarah nestled sleepily on his legs and resting on him in front, motioned his head upwards to the selection of framed photographs I had placed decoratively around the imposing antique mantle mirror above us. The photos were various shots of home with various family members stood positioned for the picture. I was in a great deal of them, and this is what Ezekiel was turning my attention to.

Merely by stating that I looked the same.

And it was true.

What had been bothering me about these photos since yesterday, though I couldn't put my finger on it then, was that they were odd. They seemed *wrong*. And it was only now that Ezekiel had pointed it out that I was able to figure out exactly what it was that was so wrong about them. In all the photographs in which I was present I looked as I do now, which most definitely should not have been so.

Some of those photographs were supposed to be pictures of myself with grandmother who died when I was only seven years old. However, instead of the younger boy who should have been in that photograph besides a 67 year old grandmother, stood 37 year old me. The same Josiah who sat peering up at them perplexedly now. And this was not the only photo to be tampered with in this way. Various others that I knew to depict me at younger ages, all held the same middle aged visage of myself.

This realisation frankly horrified me and being unable to give any explanation to this horror, I simply shook my head and sat back down in the armchair that I hadn't realised I had gotten out of to inspect the pictures since Ezekiel's statement. I was aware of my excited behaviour and could feel Ezekiel's gaze upon me as he sat on the floor, propped up against the sofa below me. I was thankful for his lack of comment and for the next hour or so we sat in tepid silence as Sarah slept soundly against her father and Ezekiel dozed awoke intermittently. The whole time I remained unmoved in my seat avoiding viewing those haunting photographs that flanked the large imposing mirror.

It was by the fourth time that Ezekiel had shaken himself awake that I heard him shuffle around and balancing Sarah in the crook of his undamaged arm, I heard more than saw him stand and stretching his long legs, briefly state that he was going to put Sarah down properly to sleep upstairs. I turned to look at him and absently gave my acknowledgement of his statement. Vacantly watching him make his drowsy way out the door, I noticed him take a step back from the threshold of the sitting room and bend slightly before disappearing into the hallway. I listened to his resonating sock-clad footsteps for a short while, as I stared vacantly out of the window until I turned my gaze to where Ezekiel had stooped down. I noticed that the boots I had placed by the doorway gone.

••••

The next day while we were sat down again around my small kitchen table, Ezekiel, who at this point had finished feeding Sarah and had his long fingers wrapped around the body of a now cooling cup of weak coffee, changed the light-hearted but ever so drab conversation we were making on the approximate size of the island and when would be a suitable time for us to go out to actually see it. This comment made me feel slightly uncomfortable, I did not enjoy going into the village main. I had no intention of making Ezekiel feel as though he were a prisoner in the house however, and readily assented. Adding that I needed to purchase more food anyway, as our current set of meals was firstly, not at all nourishing, and secondly with the 3 of us, not at all sustainable for another day.

It was decided therefore that after breakfast we would take a walk into the heart of the island. And at midday that is just what we did. With Ezekiel now wearing Dr Potter's coat and his boots firmly strapped around his ankles, he looked like every other man on the island. It was not necessarily a good look on him. I, myself was dresses similarly, though as I was prone to cold headaches this time of year, also had a thick woollen hat snugly pulled down over my ears.

Sarah was in a similar way bedecked and I was next to certain she was wearing two sets of everything under the heavy blanket Ezekiel had tucked her into. So-much-so that by the time we left, she looked like a large woollen parcel with a doll-like little face peeking out from the wrapping.

The shore directly in front of the house was as usual barren. I couldn't help but looking out to see if there was anyone else that had washed up on the beach just as

Ezekiel and Sarah had, no matter how frivolous and pointless it was. Thankfully, only the few craggy rocks that jutted out at odd intervals, my discarded boat and a few nets were all that adorned my shoreline now. I felt for the first time since living here, self-conscious in my lack of effort into making the area around my home by some means more attractive. However, a quick glance towards Ezekiel found him seemingly unconcerned with the state of the beach as we walked along. In fact it appeared as though he was attempting *not* to look in the direction of the sea at all, and had positioned both his head and body to face inland towards the grove and in the direction of the village. I'm not sure if he was aware of it, but he had also turned Sarah to face inwards so her head was facing away from the sea.

As we made our unhurried way along the worn rocky path, Ezekiel asked questions and as usual I attempted to answer them as best as I could. He seemed amused when I told him the island was named after the grove, and we kept up an amicable chat well until we got into the beginning of the denser part of the island where the majority of the population resided. We passed a few people that I was loosely acquainted with, having bought or traded from them previous times, all the while introducing Ezekiel and Sarah. The latter enjoying the multitude of attention bestowed upon her. The introductions and welcoming comments of the of the islanders, soon became passing apologies after understanding the circumstances of their arrival on the island, all of which Ezekiel brushed off with good humour and kindness that seemed inherent to him. This series of strange introductions happened with almost all whom he met. All of this in-between brief explanations directed at me of so-and-so who had moved on and was no longer trading in such-and-such good for convenience. This explained the increased number of boarded up store-fronts that seemed to have almost doubled since my last trip to the interior of the island. It also came to pass, as it so often did on the island, that many had taken up closed businesses and run them alongside their own enterprises to keep important necessities available. This I found out from Beckford the grocer I sell fish and seafood to, who had also become a barber in his backroom, as Milton who had run the hairdressers had moved on a month or so prior. I had not known. As I had no available whereas to sell that day, I purchased the extra food the three of us would need on credit and like many of the Islanders do, promised to make the return when I could. Our unique economy seemed to mesmerise Ezekiel who continuously applauded the venture the entire shopping trip.

After hours of looking around the town, greeting folks and stocking up I suggested to Ezekiel that it might be worth stopping to have lunch along the beachfront this side of the island. I explained to him that this side of the island was far more beautiful than my side, as the sea looked bluer and deeper here. There was no more light, as it was overcast everywhere on the island, but it seemed to have a brighter feeling to it then the north side. Ezekiel agreed. We now had plenty of food readily available in the thick wicker basket Beckford had placed the goods in. And the idea of a beach picnic was greeted by Ezekiel a great deal of enthusiasm, encouraged further by a litany of delicate happy babbles from Sarah, who clearly thought highly of this idea also.

••••

The beachfront we decided to stop for lunch was one close to the old tailors, which with its boarded up windows was less than an enticing scene for the afternoon, but what the drab exterior of the building lacked, the calm blue of the sea made well up for. We had no blanket to speak of so Ezekiel and I made do for seating with our jackets. And Sarah now loosened from one of the blankets that Ezekiel had wrapped her in, sat comfortably in his lap while her blanket became a makeshift table. The only food that was ready to eat was some bread, that was still delightfully warm and sweet scented, a pot of honey, a bottle of lemon drink and an assortment of fruit; including a bag of slightly gone-off strawberries which Ezekiel was eating the slightly browned bits for himself and feeding Sarah the bright red pieces.

Although the food was rather too springlike for the middle of winter, as the weather on the island seemed to almost always remain temperate, it was a passable lunch, though missing something hearty in my opinion. Ezekiel and I talked about little and nothing, and I couldn't help but feel as though the whole affair was not something we had been doing everyday for years, and not that we hadn't only just met yesterday.

Not for the first time, my familiarity with Ezekiel and Sarah both pleased and terrified me. The amicability and pleasantness felt too perfect at times and I began to worry they would soon leave as I got too attached to them. However, the thought of distancing myself from these two, though I barely knew them seemed foolish, and I worked hard to remove those unnecessary thoughts from my mind. For a few minutes I silently watched the two of them interact. Sarah now fully propped up against Ezekiel's stomach and resting on his outstretched legs, gurgled and smiled with red stained lips. Ezekiel was again dangling his golden locket in front of her as she reached up her little fat hands to reach the jewellery. The buffered links glimmered brightly in the light despite it's apparent age.

As I was close enough to observe it properly I noticed it was a delicately engraved oval shape. I couldn't make out the exact design embossed on the front from my vantage over Ezekiel's shoulder and arm, but I could tell that the work was very finely done and expensive. The thought that had been plaguing me since I first saw it, burst out and before I had fully checked myself; where had the locket come from? My question seemed to initially startle Ezekiel who at this time had had all his attention upon Sarah, but the shock was only brief and after a pause he smiled and shifted Sarah more securely on his lap by wrapping his uninjured arm around her torso and moved the hand holding the locket closer to me for my inspection.

Ezekiel's description of the jewellery was not all that surprising. It had belonged to Sarah's mother Ruth who gave it to her daughter the night she had left them. Ezekiel's tone as he said this was whimsical and rather distant. He appeared to check himself, forcing a smile into his voice when Sarah looked up at him from her perch, he gave her a short squeeze before he continued no longer facing me. He was peering down at the jewellery, with an expression that I couldn't identify, as he rubbed his thumb along and over the engravings.

As the locket was now closer, I could make out the fine carvings of flower petals and stems that made up the design. Ezekiel continued his narrative of how Ruth had worn this locket while she carried Sarah and only after her birth did she take it off. He explained in a reminiscing tone, that Ruth wore it because it held the image of her late mother, and as he had said so he pressed the small catch along the side and the small oval cover flipped open revealing a set of small photographs. The one on the right was of an amber-brown and aged hue of a late-middle aged woman that I took to be Sarah's grandmother. Despite the photographs obvious age it was a clear and well photographed visage that was the exact opposite of the photograph on the left side. The face was badly water damaged to the point that most of the features were entirely obscured to the point that if it were not for decorative up-do and the lace blouse the individual wore, I would not have been able to make out the sex at all. One thing in particular that shook me of this image was the delicate rose shaped brooch that sat pinned to the left breast of the faceless photographed woman. The brooch appeared to be of a metal with metal petals folding around a single stone. The greyscale of the photograph made the exact stone type unrecognisable, but the brooch itself was unmistakable to me as that of the very kind that Esther had worn. In fact the resemblance in the water-damaged photograph startled me so, that I had to ask Ezekiel, all the while my eyes roaming over the portrait, if this was indeed Sarah's mother. To which he confirmed, in that whimsical tone of course, that it was. The similarity in the brooch and the unsettling way that the water had obscured seemingly only the face upset me, and I drew my eyes away from the horrible object. I had to take a moment to breathe. Once calm and facing the sea once again, I began to ask Ezekiel about the night that Ruth left, only once I heard the finite click of that menacing locket shut.

Either my odd reaction to the photograph went unnoticed by Ezekiel or more likely he had chosen not to comment on my behaviour, either of which I was immensely thankful for. After a breath and without much weight to my words, I asked Ezekiel where Ruth had gone. He seemed to be waiting for the question, as laying the now dozing Sarah down on the makeshift

77

blanket, he told me as much as he seemed capable of sharing with me about his wife sudden desire to leave.

It so happened that unsatisfied with life in America, and hearing of untold liberties in Haiti, Ruth had begged the then steadfast and stubborn Ezekiel to moved the family to the Caribbean to explore the wealth of opportunities that Ruth's unnamed cousin had promised in his letter. This not being enough of a stable ground to move with a young baby, caused Ruth and Ezekiel to argue to the point that a few days after the disagreement, Ruth stole out into the night to board a ship leaving for Haiti leaving behind a hastily written and rather undetailed note and her locket behind. Through the retelling of these events Ezekiel though looked calm, paused in his retelling often and the decisive breaks in his voice were telling enough to see how the story affected him. I was honoured to hear such a tale and with a comforting hand pressed lightly on his shoulder, I told him as much. The touch seemed to reawaken his personality and he smiled once again, this time apparently entirely genuine. The smile brought a small up-tick of my own mouth and before I had well thought through the later implications,

I found myself telling this man that I had only met a day ago about Evie.

I had not told anyone about the unborn child and hardly anyone about Esther since arriving to the island. I found it easier to say nothing of my thoughts of her and only occasionally reminding myself by looking at that photograph that had stood vigil on my side-table every night for the past year. I told him hardly anything if I am entirely honest. I just said that I had a daughter, I think I did not even tell him that she had not been born. He did not ask. After a beat or so, in which I could tell he was eager to ask something, he asked where she was. The earnestness in his large eyes was halting; the left though milk white, no less earnest than the right. Usually I would have taken offence to such a question as the pain of loss was too raw, but I found I had no righteous anger in me at that point only the understanding of a man who too had lost someone he cared deeply for, regardless of the circumstances. Just as when he had first awoke I found myself drawn painfully into his gaze and distracted by the contrasting beauty of his eyes. I could only state that my little girl was gone, unable to bring myself to say much more, enthralled as I was by his earnest stare. A rather loud sneeze came from Sarah which dissipated the frisson that had formed during the silence between Ezekiel and myself, and I was both annoyed and glad of the distraction. I myself had not noticed the drop in temperature, so caught up with the emotions of our conversation. However, the light was beginning to thin and deepen and there seemed to be a soft breeze from the north that was beginning to roll in with the potential to strengthen later on. Unanimously we packed away the food we had eaten, with Sarah re-swaddled in Ezekiel's arms as I carried the groceries. We three made our way home before the evening arrived entirely and as it does so in winter, cast the island into shifting and lightless dark.

••••

That evening the light, cold rain that we walked through had turned into piercing sleet by the time we had arrived inside. About an hour or so after that, when Sarah was upstairs asleep and Ezekiel and I sat by the fire-warmed sitting room, the sleet had become fat, thick snowflakes that the wind, that had been on coming since the late afternoon, now incessantly buffeted against thin windowpanes and piled up around the window boxes.

The fire had been burning steadily for a good hour by the time the draught from under the doors and windows gave the room a chill that fought back against the intense orange that came from the fireplace. The chill deepened to the point that Ezekiel and I had both pushed our chairs closer to the heat and closer to each other to make a barrier against the cold. Since laying Sarah down to sleep, Ezekiel had joined me in front of the fire in an amicable silence that seemed to come easily from him. Though we said nothing to each other, the only sounds being the soft crackle of the logs and our own breathing that was drowned out intermittently by the wind, the quiet was more than comfortable and I found myself staring deeply into the fire and be lulled by it's hypnotic sway. Often my eyes closed involuntarily forgetting the almost, but not quite empty, cup of now freezing coffee that was loosely clasped in my hand. The sensation of warm fingers pressing against my own however woke me out of my dose. Ezekiel who was far more awake than I, had been attempting to retrieve the cup before it fell, all the while trying not to wake me. I looked over to his serenely smiling face and thanked him, to which he still smiling, simply inclined his head once and placing the cup upon the table between us, as he suggested that I sleep and that if it was alright with me he would like to stay up a little longer. I agreed and bid him a soft goodnight. As I made my way tiredly out of the room, I looked back once with my right foot posed on the first step of the stair, and I took in the warm image of the room and the two chairs pushed comfortably near the fire before I, on leaden feet made my way slowly to my lonely room.

•••

That very night sleep alluded me for the most part. Though I was pleasantly tired I felt unable to actually drift off and I lay on my side facing the drywall away from that photograph for a long time. I heard Ezekiel walk up the stairs and enter the room next door, and for a few minutes I listened as he stole around Sarah and prepared himself for sleeping. After that the house was silent again but for the deep gusts of ghoulish wind that howled through the house, and the steady lapping of water outside my windows. The snow continued to fall all through the night, and as I lay awake with the curtains drawn as I always did, the falling snow made delicate drifting shapes against the shadowy walls, and I watched them fall in that peculiar light that comes with snowfall in the darkness.

I know that I lay awake for some hours but I found that at some point I had drifted off to sleep and into a light doze, as a couple of hours or so before sunrise I was awoken from my light slumber by the soft tread of footsteps on the landing outside my room. The steps were far too heavy and spread out to be Sarah and so I concluded that it was Ezekiel awake at this dead hour. The footsteps however were not the quiet determined sort of someone getting a late-night drink, but those of someone who is uncertain where they're headed, and once or twice the footsteps faltered or stopped completely. This alarmed me to some degree as I feared should Ezekiel be sleepwalking, he may not be entirely aware of how close he was to the staircase. I was still fairly uncertain whether I should in fact intervene, Ezekiel may well have been hungry or thirsty, and I did not wish to embarrass him. However, as I finally resolved myself to get up and check, the sound of light, footsteps placing themselves on the steps came under my door, sounding evenly placed. Despite concluding that Ezekiel was awake, I quietly but hastily pulled off my covers and putting my jumper over my sleepwear, went to my door to listen further all the while avoiding the parts of my floor I knew to have loose boards.

I stood with my ear close to the wood for a few seconds but heard nothing from the stairway nor the landing. And so curious as I was I slowly twisted the knob of my door and opened it as slowly as I could, conscious of the old hinges. I poked my head out of my room and into the blackened corridor. Ezekiel was nowhere to be seen. However, a soft amber glow flickered and pulsated from beyond on the stairs, and with it the deep chill of the night. I, just as Ezekiel had before me, made my way on tentative feet to the top of the stair. However, I needn't have gone all the way to see Ezekiel stood in front of the open front door, his boots laced up and with his coat on, as he shielded the flame of the lantern from the wind outside. Upon seeing him, I placed myself around the corner of the stairwell out of sight but still able to observe him. The shielding of the lantern and Ezekiel's constant and irregular arm movements to keep the lantern out of the main force of the wind, gave me confidence to presume him fully conscious; though there was rightly no way of checking from such a distance.

 For a few moments the two of us simply stood there, he in front of the door shielding his softly glowing lantern that barely illuminated his façade enough for me to make him out. And I, who stood sneaking in the corner at the top of the stairs, observing him in my socked feet and sleep clothes. I don't know why I did not think to say anything to him. The thought of calling out to him or even to make my way downstairs and approach him to stop him from going out into the tremendous weather, did not even cross my mind. And before I had even fully understood why I was stood there spying on him anyway, Ezekiel holding tightly onto his candle stepped out into the snow, pulling the front door quietly behind him. The resounding darkness was immediately apparent. There was now no soft amber light to give some visual into the pitch, and not even considering putting on my own coat to follow, I went into the room that Sarah was asleep. I checked she was fine but still slumbering, puzzled and slowly becoming drowsy myself, I took myself back to my bed, where I slept without waking well into until the sun rose. The snow gone and the usual cold, blue-green light of morning had appeared.

• • • •

A deep and confident knocking awoke me the next day and for the first time in a long while I found I had slept well into the morning, and the light that made its way through the dismal clouds were well on their way to making midday shadows in the lonely corners of my bedroom. It appeared also that I was the only one that had overslept, as I heard the front door open and the deep familial sounds of Ezekiel's melodic voice vibrate through the floorboards.

I quickly dressed and hurriedly made my still slightly asleep way downstairs, curious to know who our morning visitor might be. I followed the clamorous sounds of shuffling and talking. I could hear a distinct female tenor mixed with Ezekiel's voice I knew then that our guest was a woman, and upon entering the cramped kitchen, I found the stooped form of Rebecca, pinching Sarah's slowly reddening cheek.

Rebecca was a sheep farmer and mother to five children who lived at the other side of the island, much closer to the town than I, and for her to have arrived at what I took to be around 11:30, must have left quite early, as she had no horse, unless she was dropped off by a neighbour which was possible. I was only loosely acquainted with Rebecca as I was with most of the islanders, but I had warmed to her kind and freckled face immediately. Since my arrival on Grove Island over a year ago, Rebecca had been one of the few, including Doctor Potter, who had consoled me warmly and made a great effort to attempt to bring me out of myself. It had only been a year, but Rebecca seemed to have changed. Her joyful spirit and wayward bright red hair had remained the same, but occasionally when I would encounter her, she seemed more and more distant and vapid. I often put it down to her stressful and ever busy life, but that morning made me really take in and notice how much she had changed since I had first met her.

Nevertheless her spirit took to Ezekiel's like two lost pennies, and their joviality lit up my small kitchen space like a pair of firecrackers. It turned out that Rebecca had heard of Ezekiel and Sarah from someone in town, and had brought along a large waxed satchel, packed haphazardly in Rebecca's way; with baby clothes and even a small pair of leather boots that were by far too big for Sarah. As Ezekiel tried to explain, but the boots were pushed back into his hands by Rebecca who emphatically and without room for argument, told him the babies *grow*.

While the two of them continued their lively chatter, I made to prepare breakfast, which was more exciting than it had ever been in my home. Ever. A whole spread of jam-lathered bread, strawberries, the usual porridge and coffee with *milk* this time. As I announced that breakfast was finished I received two astonished stares from both Rebecca and Ezekiel, who in their absorbed nattering had not noticed me walking around them. However, with a deep laugh Rebecca placed herself decidedly down on a chair that I couldn't help feel was much too small for her impressive size, and began to eat the ample meal before her with gusto, all the while thanking me for my generosity. I felt like no particular Samaritan in providing her breakfast, on top of one that she had likely already consumed, as the two of them once again reinstated their intricate but loud dialogue. While I with Ezekiel's silent assent fed Sarah pieces of strawberry and her usual warm milk in between taking measured bites out of my own repast, entirely tuning out the conversation that was happening beside me. Despite this I gathered from the snatches of conversation I had caught prior, that it was mostly Rebecca prying into

Ezekiel's life before arrival on the island. And Ezekiel squeezing out information from Rebecca likewise, about the island that he could not get from me due to my own lack of understanding and ignorance.

Truthfully I spent a good deal of that breakfast thinking about where Ezekiel had gone in the night and his obliviousness to my knowledge of his late night disappearance, made the mystery all the more alluring. My musings were only broken by the small hick-cough that Sarah made as I once again pressed a small piece of fruit to her mouth. The noise shook me out of my thoughts and I got the attention of Ezekiel, explaining that I feared I had fed her too big a piece of food. To which with his usual pleasant smile, he declared that I had done nothing wrong and that she merely needed burping, which he promptly stood and executed with efficiency.

Once Sarah was again confidently propped up in her makeshift seat at the table, Ezekiel picked up a small lilac dress that had been one of the items Rebecca had brought with her. And bringing the garment up to his chest in gratitude, turned to face Rebecca and stooped to give her a single armed hug, which I thought a little extravagant but Rebecca seemed to reciprocate heartily.

It was after this brief stint of emotion that Rebecca suggested that we should take a trip to see Doctor Potter as she had some medicine she needed to collect from him, and wondered if we might like to walk out with her. We agreed and as Ezekiel disappeared to place the baby garments in his room, Rebecca, Sarah and I waited outside on the shore; Rebecca clutching Sarah in her large arms. The weather was still bitterly cold and even though the snow from the night before had not settled, the freeze in the air was deadly apparent, making every breath produce a cloud of heat. Sarah as was now custom, was wrapped warmly in her usual two sets of blankets and was additionally cocooned in Rebecca's thick arms and her own shawl. Once Ezekiel emerged from the house, we all four made our brisk way to Doctor Potters house, as the biting cold was uninviting and we all sought the warmth of inside as soon as possible again.

The walk did not take as long as usual. Past the grove the path changed from sand and sediment to rock and grass. And leading up to the Potters, the usual flowers that bloomed a steady myriad of colour even in winter such as this, bloomed with more aggressive friendliness that day than they ever before.

 The vantage point from the Potters house was certainly something, and well before we had reached halfway up the stone path, the old doctor had opened the door and was warmly welcoming us long before we had reached its threshold. Upon greeting Graham I immediately noticed his demeanour was drastically improved. Not that he was ever a morose or depressed man, But for a man whose wife had moved on, he was startlingly joyous. His grey hair sat languidly over his head like a soft, earthly halo and his old creased face was vibrant with youth that was not overshadowed by the crows feet and sunspots. It was hard to not be appreciative of his vibrancy through the loving and fatherly approach he bestowed upon us four. I know it was felt not only by myself, as Rebecca had a warm smile on her face as she lazily sipped the floral tea he had poured us all once we were seated around his large and welcoming kitchen table. Ezekiel also had a relaxed and languid expression on his face in the presence of the Doctor, who chatted with Rebecca as he changed and checked Ezekiel's bandages.

The soft and comfort-inducing Potters home had no shortage of plush, cushion-bedecked seating that was safe for Sarah to be placed as we drank our tea. And who dozed off within minutes of being set down, in that bright home that seemed to have its own source of constant afternoon sunlight, set apart from that of the rest of the island no matter the time of day or year.

The rest of the afternoon passed in a wonderful languid, dreamlike haze, and although Rebecca had left well before evening, stating that she must return home to help her girls with making dinner, the Potter house was no less vibrant; the contentment seeming to radiate solely from Graham.

It was well into dusk before Ezekiel, Sarah and myself made our way home. We said a long drawn-out goodbye to the doctor in the frigid evening air, and made our content way down the stone-pathed hill, all the while being seen off by the silent but gently smiling figure of Graham Potter who stood in his doorway until we were lost to the thickness of the grove. Perhaps longer.

 The ennui seemed to wear off past the vicinity of the Potter house. By the time the stone turned back to sand, Ezekiel who was carrying Sarah and I, had begun to walk quickly back home. The dark was rapidly approaching by this time, and with it the lowering temperature. We longed for the proximity of the fire and hot drinks to heat our bodies. It was as we were making our quick march along the desolate beachfront, that I remembered Sarah was no longer wrapped in the addition of Rebecca's shawl, and fearing for the child I cast my gaze down to her little face as it was rested against her father's shoulder.

Her gaze however, was drawn upwards directly to the dark sky and I don't know why, but something compelled me to follow those wide eyes, and for the second time since my own arrival on the island I noticed a star peeking out from the usual curtain of clouds. It was not by any means bright, but its rarity and solitude had me entirely fixated. Just before we reached the steps that led up to the doorway of the house, I flicked my gaze down again to Ezekiel's face to see if he had noticed, but his disparate gaze stayed straight ahead and unconcerned. I did not tell him what Sarah and I had discovered.

Chapter 3

Brine

The next morning I found no one to greet me as I made my way into the cramped kitchen. On waking at my usual time just before dawn, I allowed myself a good while to lay in my bed and slowly take in the subtle changes of light that separated the night from the dawn.

I found myself lost wholly in my thoughts as I went through the generic motions of preparing breakfast. The food was identical to that of the day before, barring a fourth plate which would have been for Rebecca, who was not there. Ezekiel's lack of appearance was not alarming and wishing to allow him rest and privacy, I made a start on my own coffee and placed small dishes over Ezekiel and Sarah's porridge, as I casually tucked into my own as I stared off down the hall from my vantage point at the table.

It was only when I began to share my breakfasts with others that I noticed that I always sat in the same spot every morning. All the chairs around the kitchen table were slightly different in size, shape and colour. And I had been seating myself in the high backed, slightly reclined, wooden chair for the past year. Always with my back to the window, and the light, and staring uninterestedly through the kitchen doorway and into the dim shadows of the corridor; though now there was someone that actually might appear there.

 Although I had intended to leave Ezekiel to appear on his own, upon finishing my own porridge and coffee and removing the makeshift lid on his own, I found the food to be congealed, clumped and entirely unappetising. And as a result found myself making my way up the stairs intending to awaken Ezekiel, all the while listening out for any sound of movement that would tell me he was up. I heard none as I stopped in front of his door and carefully leant forward not quite pressing my ear to the door, but close to. I listened for a short time, and it did not take long for me to hear the soft sounds of heavy snoring reverberate from inside. It was so loud that it concerned me that I did not hear it myself first thing in the morning. The sound, I found at the time, to be rather amusing. However, as I prepared to turn and make my way back downstairs, I was arrested by the soft gurgling-coo that could only be Sarah. The sound forced me to turn again on my heel, and this time knock loud enough to be heard over the steady throaty sound of Ezekiel snoring. I received no response to this and against my better judgement and quite rashly, I turned the door handle and finding it unlocked, pressed the door open as I called out Ezekiel by name.

The room upon my entering was dark and cold. Much colder than the rest of the house. And it took me a moment to see in that heavy darkness. The thin curtains that were drawn short, were billowing softly away from the window in ghoulish shapes and swirls. Now aware of the reason for the low temperature, I turned my gaze to the bed that was pushed into the corner where the form of Ezekiel was immediately apparent. He was a large lump under the washed-out sheets. Heavy fortified and looking fairly comfortable between, Ezekiel (It was hard to tell where his head was from his feet in this way) and all the pillows, was Sarah. She seemed quite content as she was and gave me a questioning babble as to enquire why I was disturbing her. For awhile I was rather unsure as to what to do. However, it was the child again that intercepted my thoughts and reached her short arms out towards me. In all of her majesty and quietude, I approached her and made to pick her up when my eyes caught sight of a folded piece of stationary that I recognised as being my very own, from the set of draws in the desk of this very room. I put off my going to Sarah and took up the paper that lay there next to the bed. The note was addressed to me in a clear and direct hand;

Josiah,

I am glad you are reading this and I hope that Sarah is well as yourself.

Firstly, I will apologise for not informing you of my condition sooner. You will likely see, I am asleep and no sound is likely to disturb me until I awaken myself. It is a strange affliction that I have suffered with for the past three years and no medical professional has been able

99

to aid with. I am hoping that I will awake this morning and not burden you with Sarah for longer than a day.

You may be wondering how I know I would be asleep. Unfortunately I can not rightly say. This sleeping sickness tends to come in by-monthly cycles and affects me with insomnia at all other times.
I will tell you more when I wake.
Again I hope this does not last too long as I feel it may not. Until then I ask you to look after Sarah as I trust you greatly.
Your grateful friend,

Ezekiel

Quite rightly this note shocked me, and I took a minute to reread over what it said. Indeed it did make Ezekiel's late night strolling less concerning and the carefully crafted pillow cage supported the letter. I gave into a moment of curiosity once Sarah was placed in the crook of my left arm, to gently peel back the covers where I took his Ezekiel's face to be and found him to be deeply asleep. I hadn't noticed earlier, but his deep snoring had ceased and he was now breathing deeply and evenly. I watched his face for a moment and a soft slap to under my jaw from Sarah's small hand, made me place the bedclothes under Ezekiel's chin and leave the room quieter than I had arrived.

It was only as I was serving breakfast that was no more interesting than toast and coffee for myself and milky-porridge for Sarah that I wondered whether Sarah was distressed by her fathers illness. Even though she was only a baby she seemed rather aware of the events happening around her, as when I found her she seemed not at all worried, and even now seemed no worse for wear as I fed her small spoonfuls of runny oats. This led me to believe that this had happened before, and the thought fairly troubled me. I was uncertain exactly what I should do in such a case, as it wasn't everyday that strange occurrences such as I had been subject to for the past few days, happened. I cannot even remember such bizarre events happening when I was young.

I'm glad to say that I was not in fact left alone with just Sarah for too long. I think it must have only been a few hours before we were joined by Ezekiel. I remember it was late afternoon and around the time when the light changes to start creating creeping shadows in forgotten crevices.

I was sat with Sarah on the large settee. After Ezekiel's initial depositing on the couch, I had made an attempt to work out the bloodstains and moved it to sit at the window for the light, to use whatever sun may appear, to dry it. Though it was entirely dry now, two of the cushions still sported pale-pink smudges that I couldn't remove, and so covered the thing with a large throw blanket, that was completely clashing and garish. It was there that Sarah and I were sat when Ezekiel made his way into the room that afternoon.

His appearance fairly startled me, as I hadn't heard him come down the stairs and had been reading aloud to Sarah, who was sat on my lap, a book I had about old British myths and legends. A book far too advanced for her to understand a word I was saying, but the intricate illustrations that decorated the pages had arrested her attention early on and as I read, her small fat hands had been grabbing at the pages. I had long ago stopped her from covering up the words I was reading and about twenty minutes in, had begun creating fictitious stories based on the pictures, that if Sarah's giggles and grunts were any indication, she enjoyed. Even if it was only my voice she was appreciative of. And it was so that I was fairly unaware of being observed by Ezekiel until I chanced to look around and see him stood resting gently against the door jab in his shirt sleeves, and a small smile dancing across his face. He looked tired and a fairly drained, and his pleasant expression did nothing to hide the large bruising under his eyes, set off particularly by the milky film of his right eye. The cessation of my reading had Sarah stop her pawing at the pictures and turn her head up at first to me, and then cleverly follow my sight to her father. As soon as she saw him she became energetic and reached for him almost at the exact moment his own smile widened considerably, and he too reached for her.

With my legs now free I turned to place the book on the window-sill behind the settee as Ezekiel, now holding a squirming Sarah sat beside me. Ezekiel asked in his usual melodic tone if and when we were to visit the doctor as he wish to thank him again. I replied that we could go that very evening, unless he wished for some food first,. As I was aware that he had not eaten since the night before and Sarah and my own remains of both lunch and indeed breakfast, sat waiting for me to clear up in kitchen sink, rather embarrassingly. I felt guilty about it for a moment before I turned my attention back to Ezekiel who with Sarah sat comfortably in his arms, was looking at me but not in a hard focused way, but softly and expectantly. I returned his look and smiled. The smile felt odd to me. Since *that* day, it was a rare occurrence for me to be even vaguely happy about very much and as I lived alone no one was around to see my sombre expressions. Now that there were however, I became deeply conscious of my expressions.

We decided that we would go to visit the doctor that very afternoon as Ezekiel continuously asserted that he was not hungry, despite my insistent badgering. The afternoon was uncommonly bright and for the first time since my arrival on the island and I suspected and hoped that the clouds might truly clear up altogether as we three walked that gravelled path to the Potters cottage.

As the day was fairly mild, despite it being late January, I was wearing only my sweater and no coat. Sarah was still bundled up mightily and Ezekiel himself had on his back the jacket that Graham had given him. It fit him remarkably well and for a moment I tried to picture Graham the same size as Ezekiel and it took all my power to not laugh out loud. We mainly walked in silence, though occasionally Sarah would make some small noise of wonderment or appreciation at a passing butterfly or try to reach down at the lifeless white flowers that litter the ground every few paces. Ezekiel however seemed content in his own thoughts as he resettled Sarah every now and then. I left him to it mainly as ambling beside him. I had offered to carry Sarah before we had started out, as the tiredness in his face apparent despite his curious sleep the night prior. However, he merely shook his head politely, thanked me and said he was fine. The letter he had written of his strange nocturnal ailment left unspoken between us.

Once we had cleared the grove and stepped onto the path flanked by grass and weeds, my heart broke slightly at the absence of Delilah, throwing open the door. My pain must have been evident on my face, as as I stared at that lonesome cottage I felt Ezekiel's hand on my arm and met his concerned expression with my own pained one. It appeared that I had stopped as I beheld the home and to alleviate Ezekiel's concern, I began to trek up the stone path, Ezekiel and Sarah following a few paces behind. It occurred to me fully then, that I would never see Delilah again, the reality of it truly sinking in unlike the last time we were here. It was just as my eyes began to prickle with unshed tears however, that Ezekiel came beside me and matching his pace with mine, said not a word but continued our ascent up to the house.

Once we had announced our arrival through a softer and then slightly louder knock at the quaint rosewood door, Ezekiel and I shared a look. Honestly, I cannot say what was in Ezekiel's eyes, but I knew that I felt fear and concern at the lack of response; supposing the worst as I am often want to do.

Ezekiel still holding Sarah, made his way around to the front windows, and peered over the delicate colourful window boxes as he took a squinted look inside. His confused expression once he returned to my side on the stoop however, only furthered my anxiety. And through an unspoken agreement between the two of us, I pushed down gently on the door handle, not really expecting it to be open despite hoping it would be. Finding it open we stepped into the cottage.

Upon my entry what first took me aback was the absence of light. There appeared to be deep encasing shadows where I had never known them to be before, and the house lacked the smell of warmth and an emptiness permeated throughout. That is not to say that it felt dead, just empty. There appeared to be dust in places I had never once seen it before, and the coldness of the house is what shook me the most I believe. I had always known the Potters cottage to be a place of limitless warmth and health, but as we three stood there in the centre of the entryway, I could not help but feel that this house was hollow and had been forever.

Ezekiel called out, though no response came as we three waited there and Ezekiel and I shared another look, quite unsure what we were to do. I suggested that we check the house in case something had happened to the doctor. But it was as I walked around that house, that something that had not occurred to me before slowly began to creep into my mind. There was less and less furniture than I remembered. I could recall large paintings on the walls and various photographs of Delilah and Graham that used to bedeck the hallways. There were none now as I crept along the corridors.

It was only as I reached the kitchen and I heard Ezekiel pottering around in the front room (I assumed) that the airiness and the quietude of the house became macabre and rather sombre. The hallway in which I found myself was a direct parallel to the one in my own house. What disturbed my melancholy and despair at the emptiness of the house, was the soft cooing noise that was coming from Sarah. She had been quiet the whole time since we entered the house, but now I heard that she was making the same distinctive and repetitive sound over an over, as it echoed through the lonely house. Though it was mere baby talk and nothing actually consistent, I attempted to ignore it until the continued babble became more distinctive and the unintelligible word "Podder", quickly became obvious to me as an attempt at saying Graham's name.

••••

The weeks seemed to pass in a blur and I can not remember doing very much. The presence of Ezekiel and Sarah seemed to be part of my natural and everyday route, as though they had always been there as a part of my family. Though the days were rather monotonous and average, the nights however were an entirely different experience.

On Tuesday night I was awoken by a firm jostle on my right shoulder. The touch startled me from my blurry doze. I did not remember much from my dream, the memory of it seemed opaque to me; swirls of I remembered only the vast endlessness of grey and white tones that covered my vision. I remember being there but I was not sure where exactly it was. I awoke into the night to Ezekiel hunched over me in the dark. I was terrified when I awoke. The blank and sickly white of his eye, that seemed to glow horribly in the dark, was the only thing that I could make out and I recoiled slightly from his touch. I was unsure whether or not Ezekiel could see me clearly in the dark, he seemed to be aware of my flinching away from him, and perhaps he could then see me by the dim light that came in through the windows, as he stepped back slightly and waited.

I wanted to know what he was doing in my room in the dead of night and worked up the courage and hesitantly asked him. He gave me a quizzical look as if I was stating an obvious question, and rather concerned he stated that I had been screaming quite loudly for some time however, when he had come into my room I was fast asleep; tossing and turning and yelling out so loud that Sarah had woke. This surprised me, as as I said my dream were often blank and rather empty, and the fact that I had been in such a deep and restful sleep, which was peculiar for me, was further disquieting to me. I apologised to Ezekiel for disturbing him and stated that I was unaware that I had been making such a noise and if he would forgive me for waking Sarah, as I did feel extremely guilty of waking up that child through night terrors that I was apparently unaware of.

It was only as I saw him sat there in the dark, worried at my well-being that eventually the fear of his visage abated and I recognised him as a friend. I was still rather confused as to the nature of my terror as my dream were far from frightful. However, the eerie repetitive placidity of those grey and white tones that intersected and merged into one another during my dreams could become looming and engulfing and suffocating. Entering my mouth and my lungs and filling me up with despair. I could see how that could cause me to scream in reality. I was then rather grateful for Ezekiel's presence and I rather ashamed, asked Ezekiel if Sarah was asleep, to which he assured me that he had managed to put her back to sleep before he entered my room, as my screaming was intermittent.

He was crouched slightly so he could see me eye to eye as I sat up in my bed, my sheets tangled around my legs and the worry still etched on Ezekiel's face. After a moment, once he was assured that no harm had come to me, his face relaxed ever so slightly, a trace of tightness still evident. There was a brief moment of almost wordless communication between Ezekiel and I in that darkness, before he perched slightly on the edge of my bed. I was thankful, for reasons I could not rightly ascertain, that he had not left, and I sat up more fully, pulling my legs out of the sheets and sat on the edge of the bed with him shoulder to shoulder, as we sat facing the window. There was next to no light coming in through the large panes. The draught was palpable in the darkness, almost so that any light seemed tangible to us.

Though we could see barely anything, we sat there together in the dark Ezekiel's bare feet planted firmly on the cold floorboards. I wondered briefly if his feet were cold. My own sock clad feet were pressed firmly against the floor also as I pushed out the last vestiges of that disturbing dream that was not altogether disturbing from my mind.

The room was quiet. I could hear Ezekiel's even breathing as he sat beside me. His shoulders were ever so slightly hunched over and his hands hung limply between his knees. My own arms were clasped tightly around my elbows as I sat with my eyes shut in the dark. I do not know whether or not Ezekiel had his eyes open or not, but we to sat there together in the quiet, not speaking but grateful of each others company. The only sound that could be distinctly heard were the waves that crashed outside of the windows of my room. The sea was quiet that night as it had been when we had gone to sleep hours earlier, and the soft sound of the surf breaking against the shore was calming and soothing. I slowly felt my dream from before ebbing away from my conscious memory, leaving the dim light, Ezekiel's soft breathing and the sound of waves pushing up against the sand.

••••

Everything was bright. That was the first thing that I noticed. Generally speaking, sunlight did not really come into my room. It was a dreary island and the sun was always hidden behind clouds, as it was that day however, the light that was behind the clouds seemed brighter somehow, more visceral, more real and more tangible. I could feel it press insistently against my eyelids.

I came to consciousness slowly. I was aware that I was sleeping, it was one of those sorts of dreaming when you know that you've been asleep and you wish only to go back to that feeling of bliss. That was how I woke, with the light pressing down against my face.

When I awoke fully that morning, I was alone in my room. I was tucked properly into my bed, the covers tucked up under my chin and my face turned towards the light of the window, which was odd for me as I almost always slept facing the wall. As strange as it sounds, I expected to see some sort of evidence that Ezekiel had been there last night. Some impression on the bed or some lingering scent but there was nothing, and for quite some time I truly believe that I had completely dreamt his presence in my room at that strange hour. However,

114

something made me think that I was not imagining that I had awoke in the night, or the firm press of Ezekiel's shoulder against my own, and that we had in fact sat up for a very long time, saying nothing and merely listening to the sea. I don't know what it was exactly, but something told me that the experience very much happened. For a long time I lay there rather dazed and uncertain, I was vaguely aware what time it was, assuming it to be around half past seven or perhaps more closer to 8:00 o'clock. I lay there rather uncertain in those peculiarly tucked sheets that were far too neat for my usual haphazard way of wrapping myself in my bed; it could only have been done by somebody else. It was a sound that arose me from my bed. I heard through the floorboards of my room the clamour of clinking ceramic and the shrill whistling of my stove top kettle. It could only be Ezekiel, and owing to the late hour, it appeared that he was making breakfast. I hadn't expected this, and so I dressed quickly and made my way down the stairs.

 The sight that greeted me upon entering the kitchen, was exactly as I had envisioned. Ezekiel was rather at home in the kitchen, as though he had lived his entire life preparing, what appeared to be, breakfast. As I walked in two cups of coffee, one for him and I assume the other for me, sat in the centre of the table. In front of these but at a safe distance away, was Sarah. She sat propped-up against her customary books and a shallow dish of warm milk with a wooden spoon in it was perched just out of her reach. I assumed it was intended for him to feed her after he was finished preparing whatever he was doing stood at the stove. There was also a small bowl of cubed strawberries next to Sarah, who was digging her pudgy little fingers into and feeding herself with.

I stood at the threshold of the kitchen for a moment. I was grateful to Ezekiel for him taking the initiative to make breakfast, but also slightly ashamed of my inhospitality to my guests. I said nothing to Ezekiel however, and thanked him profusely for making breakfast, assuring him that he did not need to and that it was my duty to do it. He waved me off stating that it was the least he could do for me giving him board and help since the accident and indeed since his arrival. I have to admit that that day passed in quite a blur and the

116

unspoken new connection between Ezekiel and I sparked to life and pulled taut between us.

••••

I had that dream again a few weeks later. It had been about a week since Ezekiel and I had sat up that night. I had no strange dream since then, just the usual dreams of Esther and inconsequential things that meant nothing to me. I usually try not to stake too much on my dreams, preferring instead to logically interpret the things that are happening to my conscious mind. But something about this dream seems eerily unsettling in its simplicity. The same roiling clouds of dense grey and white that merge and tumble over each other and fill my senses are suffocating. They cloud my ears like cotton wool and cover my eyes. I am blinded by them. I am suffocating under them, and I cannot do anything in the midst of them. I am helpless. It appears though that I did not scream this time. I was entirely quiet and there was no Ezekiel hunched over me, attempting to wake me. If I had been screaming he had not heard me. Unlike the first time however I woke with a start this time, sweat pouring down my brow and down my chin and trickling into my ears. My shirt was soaked damp with sweat as I lay there panting for a moment, under my slowly cooling bedsheets.

For a little while I simply lay there listening to the sounds of the waves and the quiet of the house. I could not hear Ezekiel or Sarah and assume them to be asleep as it was the middle of the night by my guess. After about half an hour or so of laying there I decided to get up. I had nothing in mind to do I just simply had an urge to move. To be somewhere else. I made my way over to the window intending to just look out into the dark and dim light. It was that time of the night where the pitch dark had fully gone and now there was only a navy tinge to everything, not quite bright enough to see, but enough to make out distinct shapes and shadows along the beach front. I could see my boat bobbing up and down and the soft swell of sea, and I could see the distinct colouring of the sand in contrast to the sea and indeed the sky.

I don't know how long I stood there just staring out into that contrasting clouded sky that overshadowed all, and I was almost hypnotised by the drab and lifeless edge of the island. And it was only as I was staring so very blankly, that I noticed a figure along the beach front. It should have worried me that a figure was heading towards the house at this hour. By all rights I should have been afraid that it was some sort of robber or perhaps another washed up soul, but things like that did not frequently happen on the island. Ezekiel and Sarah were rare occurrences, and so I just stared intently. I knew the door to be locked, and there was only one door that led into the house. All the windows were closed and half of them did not even open; barred shut from years of disuse and so it was that I just stared at this figure.

It was the gait of the person as they got closer that became recognisable as that of Ezekiel. This do not shock me as I had seen him leave out on that night in the middle of that storm, and part of me sort of thought it might be him anyhow. However, he was coming back this time, returning from wherever he had been. I felt a

119

strange feeling in my stomach watching him in the night, moving like some sort of wraith indistinguishable from the rest of the shadows unless one was looking as intently as I. At breakfast the next morning, I did not bring it up.

••••

The same motions of the kitchen in the mornings repeated without hitch for months and became monotonous. Ezekiel and I moved around each other in a common almost well practised symphony and Sarah sat at the table seeming to get bigger and bigger everyday, though only three months had passed since the initial arrival of the two of them on the island. It felt sometimes as though we had been here living together for years.

Something about Sarah and Ezekiel was heart-wrenching for me. Sarah in particular. Though I tried to put the similarities of my own lose child out of my mind, there were days when I could not ignore how close to being my true reality, if that accident had not happened, our situation was.

120

That morning I was feeding Sarah. We were running out to food and would soon have to go back into town to fetch more. I noticed in the strawberries that I was feeding Sarah, I was picking out more and more bad bits and leaving her only with the brightest, freshest red pieces of fruit, that did not seem like enough. The milk also was running out, and Ezekiel and I had an unspoken agreement to have milk-less coffee that morning, preferring to give Sarah the entire remains of the milk. I was sat comfortably in my customary spot in my high-backed chair picking out slightly browned pieces of strawberry when Sarah, in between her usual messy eating and babbling, began to repeat the phrase she had used when were at the Potters cottage the day before. The continuous and childlike botching of Potter's name brought a smile to my lips and I could tell also that Ezekiel was pleased with Sarah's improvement in speech, at one point in-between feeding I had to stop entirely as she kept babbling on. It was then that the sounds Sarah was making changed all of a sudden. Sarah was no longer trying to say Potter, but what sounded like "ozai-ah" or "osay-a". She said it again, and then again, looking at me the whole time as she slammed her small palms down on the wooden table, smiling and giggling as she did.

I had stopped feeding her at this point and gave her a quizzical look which she completely ignored and continued babbling and screeching and repeating her strange "osaya". I was rather confused and I looked to Ezekiel who was shovelling watery porridge into his mouth, as though He did never be fed again. He looked up at me rather bashfully and I gave him a quizzical look again, and after he put the last spoonful of porridge into his mouth, he placed his spoon down and sat back in his chair. The light of the window shone brightly into his face and reflecting off the creamy white of his right eye.

He looked at me for a moment, an indulgent and (I thought) rather embarrassed smile on his face. I was even more confused and it was only as I took in Ezekiel's strange expression and Sarah's continued babbling, that I realised that Sarah was saying my name. The baby talk made it incomprehensible and almost impossible to ascertain what she was trying say from the vowels she was using. I turned back to Sarah and

122

looking deep into her large eyes. I spoke to her, more as you would speak to an adult than a baby, asking if she was attempting to say my name. The most substantial answer I received in return was a loud giggle – a baby's equivalent of a belly laugh – and the continued repetition of my new name. I smiled and turned to Ezekiel who had got up to deposit his bowl and spoon in the sink. He had his back to me but the window pane clearly reflected the smile that was plastered on his face, as he admitted he had been trying to teach Sarah how to say my name late into the night when I was asleep after the incident at Potters cottage. At this point he turned around with bashful but happy smile still pressed on his face. I couldn't help but laugh myself and lean back in my chair as Sarah in-between saying my new name, was mashing her fingers into the bowl of strawberries in front of her. The situation was hilarious and I couldn't help let out a deep laugh. It was sharp and quick but no less gleeful. Ezekiel himself found it funny also and he made to clear up the breakfast things that were no longer being eaten, including the mush that Sarah had now made in the bowl. I stood to help and he waved me off claiming that as I had made breakfast it was only right that he clear it up – I acquiesced and sat back down. I made to wipe Sarah's mouth in-between her giggles and intermittent repeating of my name, and Potter's occasionally, as she wiggled and squirmed away from the cloth. Whilst I was sufficiently distracted, Ezekiel bent towards the table from my right side and lay a piece of stationary down on the surface in front of me. I turned my eyes away from Sarah and looked up at him confused. He glanced at the letter and then looked away out the window. I thought his behaviour odd, but I waited for his explanation.

I took in the letter as he spoke; it was an address that I did recognise but was postmarked to go to London, it was only missing a stamp he said, it was a letter to his sister explaining that he was alive and everything that had happened since he had left America. I am ashamed to say it but something in me lurched at the thought of that letter. The possibilities that it held. The future that I had no control over, and for a dirty long minute I despised that letter and I despised Ezekiel. I knew then that he would not stay on the island with me forever, with Sarah. I had grown so accustomed to their presence and so used to them, that the thought of him contacting his sister and the possibility of them leaving set a deep and ugly pit in this bottom of my stomach and wrenched at my heart. On the outside however I simply agreed with Ezekiel and told him I would put a postmark on it. I had a packet of stamps somewhere in this house and I would send it out where we next went into town, I said. He thanked me and placing a hand on my shoulder went to pick up Sarah. As he left the room I heard him call back, his voice travelled down the corridor and claimed that he was going to get Sarah properly ready for the day. I assume that I must have called back some assent as I sat there in my seat at the kitchen table, staring down at a letter that would now ruin my life.

I don't think that it is a shock to know that I did not send the letter. I simply could not physically. I went for an early walk the next morning and before leaving, I checked Ezekiel and Sarah's room beforehand to make sure that he was definitely in, and put the letter into a hidden pocket in the lining of my coat, which had been there for as long as I could remember. When I returned and prepared breakfast, I lied to Ezekiel and I told him that I had packed it onto the post-boat and it would arrive on the mainland the next day.

Those lies were integral.

They were essential to the survival of our relationship.

It was something that needed to be done and I am glad I had the strength to do it. It would take more strength to let them go and leave me here alone once again. Evie can live again through Sarah and I will have my daughter, and if necessary Ezekiel can be removed. My Evie was taken from me far too soon. It's not fair that he should have his daughter and I lose mine

Chapter 4
Dilute

 I had never been to the grove at night; and even during the day, never off the beaten down gravelly path. It may seem strange, but I suppose I never really had much reason to actually venture in there. I tended to be a homebody most of the time living alone on the island. I only ever really went out to half-heartedly fish once in a while, and I especially never once thought to leave out in the dead of night to go and explore the potential hidden secrets of the grove. However, Sarah and Ezekiel's presence on the island had upturned and rearranged quite a many things that would have likely remained unchanged in my unvaried life, had they not arrived. And it was due to this, that I found myself alongside Ezekiel ambling through that long-standing and until now, unexplored grove in the dead of night.

Exactly why we were there, was due to Ezekiel's wanting to see the grove properly, so he said, and though it would probably have made more sense to take Sarah, she had been deposited in Rebecca's safekeeping for the night, at her insistence that Ezekiel needed a break. A comment which to my surprise he readily agreed to, despite not knowing Rebecca as long as I had. I found myself judging him slightly then, despite my own trust in Rebecca.

For this particular trek into the grove, it seemed like he wanted to be without her. I'm sure that's too harsh a thing to say, but it seemed as though he wanted to be alone despite his unwavering urgency in inviting me. Though looking back at that bizarre conversation, he did not really invite me in so many words. It was more that he asked if I had ever been to the grove at night, to which I could only answer in the negative. And that was how we found ourselves at 3 o'clock in the dead of night in that eerie, luminous dark that came with nighttime on the island, stepping out with two cloth covered lanterns. The ability to see without the an exact external light source, gave the low lit and hollow night an odd sensation. The two of us bundled up in our jackets, scarves and woollen hats, out taking a walk in the middle of the night, that was simultaneously extremely bizarre and yet so natural.

The walk to the grove was cautious. Despite our large lanterns we could not see anything with any exactness as the clouds entirely covered the sky, and what moonlight there would have been was completely hidden, but the strange almost-darkness that came with night time on the island prevailed, though weakly. Our lanterns gave out twin barely-there flames that we used to see only where we were placing our feet and no further.

To the right of me I could hear the breaking of the waves against the shoreline, it was the same muted and soothing sound I did heard for the past year and a half living on that island, and it had become so much a part of my senses that it became a part of every thought and sound that I made, to the point that in that unsettling night it soothed me. The breaking waves erased any fear and trepidation I had previously felt walking in that almost-twilight; and with Ezekiel beside me I had the courage to continue on.

It's hard to say exactly what Ezekiel felt walking with me, as he was very quiet the whole time and it was only as we were lighting the lanterns and stepping out that he gave me a brief smile and a nod, since then he had not spoken. However, he seemed at ease and I did not want to ruin his contentment by saying nonsensical things, and so I kept quiet.

It was only as we reached the edge of the grove that Ezekiel spoke. He rather bizarrely asked me what type of flowers or weeds grew inside the grove, and I was of course obliged to respond that I did not know, having not really paid much attention to such things, and would have been unable to understand the difference even if I had.

It was not through sight that alerted me that we had got to the grove, but the change in texture underneath my boots. The gritty crackling of shale and sand changed to soft yielding moss and soil. The dichotomy between these two textures was astounding even in the daytime, when the washed out beige and grey of the shoreline clashed harshly with the deep greens and browns of the grove. Now though in the near darkness the grove felt close, and I could tell we were within the line of trees, due to the lack of openness that came with it. It made me wonder briefly if Ezekiel felt the same, as he stopped beside me. I could not see his expression as he was a good foot shorter than me, but his silence seemed almost to be in exultation at the nighttime beauty of the grove.

The trees seemed to swallow up the light that our lanterns gave out, and only succeeded in illuminating a metre of so into the trees, the rest of it was almost pitch black. Despite the usual lack of diverse fauna on the island, that was not weeds or those insipid white flowers, the sounds from the grove were fascinating. The twittering and scurrying of small animals and roaming nighttime birds were astounding to me as they could not to be heard from my house, nor even along the shoreline.

131

Here in the grove however, the sounds suggested a wide range of life, into being.

After a moment of taking in the strangeness of the grove at nighttime I turned towards Ezekiel, he seemed just as enraptured as I was, stood at the tree line; irreverent and almost as though he wished not to step over it. I thought this odd but nonetheless I took a step forward myself, daring him almost follow me. I turned around and observed Ezekiel, a playful smile passed over his face that I mirrored as he too stepped away from the tree line and followed me in.

We walked for a while, perhaps no longer than 10 minutes in the dark, all the while our lanterns giving out meagre unsubstantial light. Frequently we tripped into each other as our feet caught on large sticks and twisted twigs that lay in our way. However, there seemed to be an unspoken agreement for us to continue, neither of us seeming to want to turn back. I found myself steadying Ezekiel's slighter frame occasionally. When he tripped over what I assumed to be the fallen tree stump here or there, he pitched forward and I could only really see his hand flail in front of my lantern as his own light moved haphazardly and erratically as he fell, before I grabbed onto his arm and yanked him backwards towards me; preventing is fall. Though he laughed good-naturedly and thanked me profusely, I could tell that he was rather shaken and I suggested to him that we sit for a moment and find somewhere we could rest ourselves. Though I hesitated to say it, I did suggested we turn back. Ezekiel however seemed not to like the idea and shaking his head, though I could not see but only feel the motion of his head moving beside me, continued on in a more steadfast pace seeming unwilling to relent to the night. And I followed after him. What happened next was bizarre.

We had walked for around half an hour, when the light seemed to change slightly. It was getting later on in the night and closer to dawn, around 4 o'clock most likely, it was hard to tell. As I have said before, the light on the island is queer; it tends to stay at a vaguely twilit hue at night and only really gets fully dark for around an hour or so. And in the grove full of trees with crooked and obscure shapes, the brain plays tricks. It's natural to not be able to see perfectly in low light and dense forest for many people, but what I saw was unmistakable. Now that the hour of fully dark had past and the early twilight was creeping in, I could see a little more clearly than before. Straight ahead, there was not quite a clearing, but more like a gap in the tree line, with perhaps seven or so trees flanking us on the path on either side leading up to where this gap was. And it was obvious that it was not a tree or a large deer we had no deer on the Island nor could it have been a bird, as it was too big.

What it looked liked, was a person from a distance.

But why would somebody be in the grove with us at this hour? I was about to alert Ezekiel that we had come across somebody else, it was rare but I thought it would be worth saying something to him should he be alarmed or whatever. However, it was just as I was about to say something and we were getting closer to this person or apparition even, that the face came into view.

134

I have very good eyesight and always have. The figure was as though Esther was stood there not a few metres off. I know this is so strange. I do not believe In ghosts. I don't believe that the undead come back, but I can say with utter certainty that it was Esther that was stood in that clearing. Her face looked just as I remember it, it was astounding and I rushed towards her.

I remember Ezekiel grabbing my arm I think, but he was too slow and I had already moved off into the dim light towards this figure who as I neared, turned and fled.

I chased after her, as she was not dead for a moment!

In that moment, I truly thought she was not dead.

It seems that some part of me at the time was aware but unconcerned, that as I shrugged off Ezekiel I seemed to have pushed him slightly, and he lost his footing and fell. I heard the impact of his body hitting the ground and I also heard him yell after me, but I ran still.

135

I ran after her because it was Esther. For a brief moment, whatever it was looked so much like her.

You will think I have not grieved properly and that is why I chased after an apparition in a forest, pushing my friend over, unknowing whether he had have seriously hurt himself or not, thank goodness he did not follow immediately.

I chased this thing for sometime, until what I saw in front of me became less and less like a person and more like a flinting shadow. The dense light made me see the shadow of the figure, nothing more than that. I couldn't tell you what she was wearing or how her hair was positioned. I was chasing after a shadow it seemed. I don't know when it was exactly, but I began to realise that I was doing just that – I was chasing after her shadow.

I remember consciously slowing my breathing as my steps faltered and the shadow winked out. I remember quite clearly seeing the apparition disappear, as I stood in the middle of the grove in the middle of the night alone. Weakly I held the lantern as big, fat pathetic tears trailed down my face. The saltiness of them as they dripped across my lips and fell onto my boots made me feel weak and powerless, as I stood in that grove and I cried to myself; a shadow that had run off in one direction and a fallen friend in the other. I felt so bad at the time, and was so entirely wrapped up in my head that I was completely unaware that Ezekiel had made his way over to me. It was the soft crunching of his boots against the ground that alerted me to his presence, but he must have been walking towards me for some time. I hesitated to turn around, I had after all pushed him over to chase after the ghost of my dead wife. I did not want to turn around and see the look of pity or disgust on his face, and so I stood there hunched over with tears racking my body.

Ezekiel said nothing as he stood behind me. I could hear that his breath sounded heavy, and I felt his hand touch me lightly on the shoulder. It was a simple and thoughtful gesture, he had not spoken but he was *there* and I was immensely grateful. After a moment I turned myself around, ashamed of my childishness in at first not turning to him, but with the sight that beheld me, oh how I could have cried once more!

His head through the amber-toned night – though perhaps at this point it was more like a dawn light – had a large gash across his left brow, where thick clots blood stuck in stark and horrific contrast to the milky and dense white of his eye. He seemed like some sort of ghoul to me in that light and the horror must have shown on my face for he smiled slightly, and that smile was more than enough to remind me that this was no daemon – this was my friend and I had hurt him. He reassured me in his usual placid tone that he was fine. He was comforting me after I was the one that had attacked him in a brief fit of hysteria! He that was assuring me that it was *alright*. In that moment I was never more than happy to have had him wash up on my shore. I was as I say immensely grateful for Ezekiel's presence, no words were fitting to apologise for my behaviour and all I could really do was stare as he stared back at me. I could see the acceptance and forgiveness in his eyes despite the blood trickling down into his only good eye – making him close it slightly. I fished out the handkerchief that was in my pocket and cleaned away the blood that was trickling into his eye and dabbed at the blood along his forehead. He blinked his eye open and smiled with thanks. As I pressed the handkerchief towards the epicentre of the wound he winced slightly but accepted the cloth with thanks and pressed it against his head himself.

We stood there for a moment quietly contemplating our strange position. It was then that I felt a slight patter of rain against my cheek that slowly began to increase, we quickly looked around in all directions for some sort of shelter that we could take. The obvious and easiest decision would likely to have been to return home, as we were only around 10 away from the house and could easily have turned back, but as we stood there contemplating the rain increased heavily and we were forced to take shelter under a large crop of trees that had bent down to give some shelter.

We stopped there for quite some time, the trees gave ample shelter and only a few drops of water landed on my jacket. We were dry and that was what was most important, we had no rush to get back home so we sat there on the slightly damp cold earth together basking in the bizarreness of the night.

The rain clouds had fully covered the sky and had created a dark atmosphere that made the dim light dimmer. The presence of Ezekiel was comforting even though in the low light it was mostly only his blind eye that seemed to shine out.

I thought that we would be fairly content to sit there not speaking, but Ezekiel shuffled slightly and quite out of nowhere he began to tell me dreams that he had when he was in his deep sleeps. It turns out that he often dreamt about his wife Ruth returning to him and Sarah, not in a good way though, she always came as some sort of wraith in the night to steal back their daughter and take her far away somewhere that he couldn't reach. He admitted that those disturbing dreams were often the reason that he did not sleep well, and he suspected that the trauma of Ruth leaving as she did was what caused the sleeping problems that he had, as they only seemed to have started once she had left.

I felt pity for Ezekiel and could not imagine what it must feel like to be abandoned by somebody you love intentionally. In Esther's case she had no say and neither did my child. I felt unworthy to offer him very much more support, after all I did try to abandoned him in the woods in search for a wraith. Instead, I told him that he was a good man and that no one would take his daughter from him. I'm sure he missed Ruth dearly, but it was clear that she was not a good wife or mother. I did not say this to him however, instead I shuffled ever so slightly closer to him and rested my shoulder against his as as show of fraternal support, as the rain petered out.

••••

The next day Ezekiel's small head wound, that though had bled profusely the day prior, had stopped bleeding but there was a small gash just above his left eyebrow. Sarah seemed to notice it as she kept grabbing at his face, but Ezekiel seemed no worse for wear and I had changed the bandage on his arm when we had arrived home. Rebecca had been waiting for us – as I tended to leave the door open – with Sarah sat on her lap as she played with her. Rebecca had also brought one of her daughters with her, I which one, as there were so many of them; they seemed to multiply year by year.

By some unspoken agreement that day, once Ezekiel had thanked Rebecca and I had given Rebecca's daughter some strawberries to take back with her and she and her mother had left, we decided that the three of us would return to the grove in the day. Unlike during the night, the sky seemed unlikely to rain.

We packed a small lunch that consisted of some sandwiches on ever so slightly stale bread for Ezekiel and I, as well as a carafe of coffee, and a small bottle of milk as well as a repurposed sugar box full of strawberries for Sarah. The day was crisp and slightly warmer than it usually was, so that I carried my jacket with me but slung over my shoulder, the basket of food in my other hand. I felt uneasy looking Ezekiel in the eye. Ezekiel however, seemed unperturbed of the events of the day before and was chatting along beside me, seemingly unconcerned with what happened yesterday. I was thankful for Ezekiel's behaviour in regards to the incident and though I knew I had to talk to him at some point about what happened I felt like he understood me and I thought there was really no need for me to say very much, after all how could he possibly understand fully what it felt like to lose both your wife and your daughter on the same day? Ezekiel had only lost his wife – he still had Sarah.

The walk into the grove was less eventful than yesterday. I saw no apparition and felt no need to chase off after shadows with some sort of madness this time however. For a while we three ambled around in the grove; Ezekiel picking flowers for Sarah and waving them in front of her face as she grabbed at them, and I walked along beside them not really having very much of a role to play at all. We wandered for a bit until we found a quite comfortable clearing that I had never noticed before. Ezekiel heading straight in that direction and I couldn't help but think he was aiming for this place all along, most likely finding it on one of his late night walks, or perhaps the night before.

We sat around much like we did a few weeks ago on the beach, as we ate and chatted about nothing in particular – facts about the island, about Sarah and about Rebecca and all the other people who lived on the island. We avoided the topic of our pasts entirely, quite content to just act as though they did not exist. It felt like one of those days that the sun ought to be shining; twinkling off the leaves and branches and illuminating the place. But the grove was as it always was; light glistened bright as ever but through a haze of cloud.

Despite the comfort of our little setting I felt out of place and jilted. Though the Grove did not seriously present very much of a disturbing feeling for me, after the day before I couldn't help but feel slightly exposed and uncomfortable. A feeling that seemed to go completely unnoticed by Ezekiel who was enjoying chittering to and playing with Sarah. That is until Sarah began to yawn and Ezekiel, who was propped up against the large oak that he was resting against, settled her more

144

comfortably as she began to fall asleep. He looked over towards me and smiled then. I couldn't help but blurt out everything that had been going on in my mind since yesterday.

I told him about what I thought I had seen in the treeline, about my hesitance to follow it but my certainty that it clearly must have been my wife. I told my story in a rush fearing that he would think me absolutely mad. He did not and I was immensely grateful as he just gave me his usual understanding polite smile and I couldn't help but smile back at that beautiful face, it was almost ethereal.

I have to admit that telling Ezekiel my story of the day before had relieved quite a weight off of my mind and I relaxed against the tree trunk next to him, my shoulder propped up against his and my head resting just above his own against the thick bark of the tree. I was comfortable and I was content and I could see clearly that Ezekiel was as well, by the warmth of the soft baby that was laying on his lap. I myself couldn't help but feel comforted by the release of my burdensome thoughts, and with the warmth of Ezekiel laying next to me, before I knew it I was following Sarah into drifting off to sleep.

It was a strange sleep sort of sleep that felt as though I was aware that I was asleep, and I enjoyed the comfortable feeling. It felt as though it ended all too quickly though, and eventually I stirred and fully awoke. When I woke the light had changed. There was still that eerie brightness of the island afternoon, but I could tell that the light had shifted and it was a little bit later on – perhaps three or four o'clock in the afternoon. There was a slight wind now too that hadn't been there when we had left out. I felt the breeze more distinctly as I did not have my jacket on, as it was on the ground and overlapping with Ezekiel's jacket to make a makeshift blanket for the two of us. I felt content despite the slight chill and I did not wish to get up. I could not really move my head to see if Ezekiel was asleep, but I could tell that he was at least dozing as he was snoring softly. Not as loud as he had been a few weeks ago, but he was breathing deeply – sort of like when he had first washed up on the island and I had him in my sitting room.

I shifted my head slowly so that I could look at him properly as he lay beside me with Sarah still perched comfortably in his lap. She had moved slightly in her sleep, and her face was turned towards me; her little arms and fists were bunched up. When I had fully turned my gaze to Ezekiel, I could not help but be once again struck by the unearthliness of his face. Though his beauty was mostly obscured by his closed eyes, his face was nonetheless graceful. The soft jut of his chin and the highness of his cheekbones flattered the even tone of his skin. I was in awe at how well made he was. His slender body was a princely contrast to my own. I felt brutishly enormous in comparison and I couldn't help but feel that should Shakespeare's Oberon exist, he would take the exact likeness of Ezekiel in that moment. And in that same moment I couldn't help but think that he would make a beautiful corpse.

I think I had had this feeling before when he had washed up along my shoreline and I saw his form laid out amongst the surf and the wreckage that had come with him. I hadn't given it much thought after that, as majority of my mind was concentrated on reviving him and letting him settle into the island with Sarah. It was at that moment, while I was remembering this that the letter that was still in my pocket felt as though it had burned my chest slightly. I had forgotten that it was even there until that point and my act of selfishness to keep Ezekiel and Sarah with me seemed further justified in that moment. Who would not want to keep something as pristine as Ezekiel and Sarah with them when they were so damaged, corrupt and abandoned themself?

In that moment all I could think of was that Ezekiel was a being that belong to me. He was something precious, something that was wronged but untainted by the harshness of the world. He was as though a bright new flower had blossomed on an old decrepit plant, and I couldn't help but feel that if he was to live any longer in this world he he would become a withered yellow leaf. I don't know exactly what compelled me to do it, I think it was perhaps a complex mix of fear, jealousy and devotion to him, but I felt myself moving, just as I had moved my head before, in an achingly slow way. I moved my arm, the one that was not pressed against

148

Ezekiel's own, it was an almost unconscious movement actually. I don't think I was really thought very much of it when I was doing it, but I felt my hand move almost of its own volition towards Ezekiel's face. I had no intention truly of what I was doing and before I really could comprehend, I had placed the palm of my hand over his delicate nose and across his well shaped lips, impressed my fingers into the soft flesh of his cheek. Surely something as beautiful as Ezekiel had no right to live in a world such as ours. I stared into his sleeping face as my hand covering his nose and mouth gently, and did not press down I just held it there savouring moment.

I leaned forward, so far forward in fact that I could feel my own breaths ricochet off his face and back into my own skin. I breathed in the scent of him for a moment before I began to press down against his face, covering his airway. There was no urgency in my movements, it was a slow and sensual action.

I did not want to rush it.

I did not want to him to struggle.

I wanted him to accept that this is where we would be always – the three of us. but something in me made me pull my hand back. I don't know what it was, I just stopped. I pulled my hand back and Ezekiel began to stir slightly, as though he was having the most pleasant dream and was upset to be interrupted. For a moment I thought he had been awake the whole time and was stalling. But his awakening seemed genuine. I sat back fully and moved away entirely from Ezekiel, the warmth of him leaving my body fully as he began to wake up properly.

It took us a few moments to ready ourselves. Ezekiel appeared completely unaware of what had happened, and Sarah could be no witness to my actions as she was still asleep after all. I alone with the trees knew exactly what had transpired in the past few minutes before Ezekiel had woken properly.

I stood and stretched out my limbs and paced around the little clearing as I looked deep into the growth; somehow self-conscious. I suppose the guilt that I did not feel earlier was emerging. It's not unusual I thought, to become self-conscious if you attempt to kill a man who has been lodging in your house without reason.

I watched him for a moment as he softly rubbed the sleep out of his eyes. I couldn't help but be slightly nervous to think that he had felt my hand on his face, perhaps even he could smell something of me lingering on his face.

I reached for Sarah so Ezekiel could stand and stretch out his own legs. She was still asleep but I walked around with her for a little bit, trying not to jostle her too much so she would stay asleep and comfortable. Once Ezekiel was done stretching he picked up both of our jackets and dusted them off from any debris that might have been on the ground, there was hardly any and so he shrugging on his own jacket as he offered me mine. I slung it over my shoulder with my free hand, avoiding jostling Sarah too much.

I watched Ezekiel pack away the remains of our lunch and once he had finished, he stood with the basket in his arm and looked at me enquiringly. I suggested we walked to the Potters hill as I thought it might be nice, and in agreement Ezekiel followed me through the grove. The walk was rather pleasant and Ezekiel told me of a strange dream that he had something about grass and walking barefoot. I absent-mindedly said it sounded nice.

Sarah awoke when we reached the edge of the Potters land, she gave a rather large yawn and snuggled further into my arm, though she stayed fully awake, and Ezekiel reached to touch her softly on the head. At the edge of the grove the Potters cottage looked as lonesome as I had ever seen it and I couldn't help but smile sadly. The absence of the loving Potters seemed to make the island feel smaller and more isolated. I was glad in that moment to have Ezekiel. Ezekiel seemed to radiate in himself the warm space and fresh air that Potters and their home did. I watched him stood there at the edge of the grove exhale and inhale. Breathing and alive.

We stood there at the floral barrier where the flowers turned from white to a mirage of colours, and Ezekiel bent down to pick a small bunch of peculiarly large forget-me-nots. He placed the few flowers into a small bundle and tucked them inside Sarah's bonnet. He stood back to admire his work with a mock-stern look on his face, and Sarah giggled happily, glad to have nice accoutrement to her usual attire. Or perhaps just happy to have her father's attention. I smiled down at the baby that was entirely unaware that I had tried to kill her father only twenty minutes ago. When I looked back up to Ezekiel he was staring at me rather churlishly, he had a goofy expression on his face and brandished a small bunch of forget-me-nots at me. The dainty blue flowers gleamed with dew in the light, their petals seemed so very delicate in his hand – the very life of them ripped out the moment that he plucked them – the taking of life for *me*. I stared at him for a moment. I believe that he thought he had made me awkward or uncomfortable. He was just as much as a killer as I was – if not more. I leant forward and with my free hand that was not holding Sarah, I pointed to my breast pocket and watched as his nimble fingers placed the flowers delicately into my jacket pocket.

••••

Later that evening as I was sat on the edge of my bed in the almost darkness that shone unobstructed through my bedroom window, I removed those small forget-me-nots from my pocket. I placed the flowers next to the photograph of Esther that stood vigil on my nightstand. I murmured a silent lament to her and asked for her forgiveness. I knew she would understand however, she always understood me. She always forgave. It was only at that point that I realised that the forget-me-nots were almost the exact same shade of blue she used to love. The same colour as that ribbon. That day I missed Esther more than ever. Had she ever truly left me?

PART II – ANCHOR

Chapter 5

Soak

10 years earlier

I think I was a disappointment to my father – if the frequent visits of his fists that were impacting my head every evening that he downed a bottle of something or other, were any indication. My mother was never very good at standing up to him either. Honestly, I don't think she ever really cared. She was a woman who was more interested in money and material gain than love.

You see my father and mother were tobacconists, well that was their official business, but they sold all sorts of things from knick-knacks and everyday items to alcohol and tobacco. Mostly it was sort of like a grocers. We lived along the wharf and my mother was the main shopkeeper as my father enjoyed going off on extraordinarily long trips to pick up specialised tobacco. We all really knew that he was visiting prostitutes down in the bigger cities, but my mother cared very little as to what he did when he was away.

I was an only child and my father felt that beating on his only son was a good way to keep him in line. Almost every night my father would come home from a night of endless drinking to drink more still at home and when he remembered that he had a son, he would lash out – all the alcohol fuelling his disappointment and resentment me. Why he seemed so intent on bullying me I could never ascertain. I worked in the shop, just like I'm sure my parents had intended when they had opened the family business that had been passed down from my grandfather, but I think there was some sort of expectation for me to do better. My father could never put into words his feelings for me and so instead he put it into violence.

It is fair to say then, that as a young man my face looked rather awful. I was never that handsome; I had a dull, ruddy complexion that added a strange hue to my skin that was already a sickly washed-out brown colour. With the artful fists of my father, this colour was intermingled with darker splodges from the bruises that were left behind.

I left school once I realised there was nothing there that would really benefit my future and my parents did not seem to care either way, despite having a lot to say about how useless I was, but never very much to say about the part they played in their overall lack of interest in me. I couldn't help but think that if I had been born a girl they would have show much more interest in me.

One particular evening when I was the ripe age of seventeen, I limped upstairs to my room. My nose was a mess of congealed blood and I was missing my second molar. By this time I had lost three of my secondary teeth to my father's wrath. I sat on the small rickety bed in my attic room and for the first time since I was nine years old I cried. I can not say exactly what it was that made me breakdown. I suppose my father had been hitting me since I was old enough to look him squarely in the eye, but I had never cried before that night. Deep, muffled and body-wracking sobs left my mouth as my nose dripped with blood and snot. Saliva edged out my lips uncontrollably, mixing in a lurid stream of pinky-red down my shirt and onto my trousers. I struggled to hold my cries in. My forearms were bruised from the boots that had impacted with the flesh moments before, and no one could hear me. My mother, my father and I were the only occupants in our house, and my room being at the very top of the house and they being at the very bottom, meant that we were so far apart the gunshot probably would probably not rouse them. They would not really have cared, if they had heard me crying anyway. That night I cried for a long while before I passed out.

I woke up in the middle of the night, cold and with a bloody pile of drool next to my face. I had collapsed on top of my thin covers, fully dressed. Almost robotically I changed my clothes – throwing the old ones in a pile on the floor. I placed the only thing that really ever gave me any pleasure in my pocket. It was a small black and gold gilt-bound notebook and a small golden pencil that fit into a catch on the side of it. It had been a present from my aunt when I was younger and I managed to save pages by only writing down essential thoughts in clipped shorthand that only I understood. I placed this gift in my jacket pocket, along with the ten pounds which I had stolen from my father a month ago. He had no idea about it, due to his almost constant state of drunkenness. If anyone was to know, it would have been my mother; but I did not care what she thought.

I made no attempt to conceal my footsteps as I made my way down the stairs – if anyone had heard me I doubt they would have cared much. So I walked down the stairs from my attic room, along the first landing, opened the door to the next set of stairs that led down into the shop and out into the empty street. In that moment I believed that if I simply just kept walking nobody would know I was missing, and nobody would care. Some part of me was petty and thought I was probably doing them a favour. A part of me wanted to turn back and make both of their lives as miserable as possible. But I resisted the urge to turn back, knowing that my mother would be stood probably from my bedroom window watching her only son leave his home in the middle of the night. Her own black eye swallowing up the light from inside the shop as she silently watched him walk away.

For a very long while I meandered around the ports, taking up basic dockside work. I was never very any good at it, but I had strong, solid hands, and the supple muscle that I did picked up through my teenage years was put into good use hauling crates and the like off of ships and into storage. I did this for perhaps two or three years. I remember that I always coveted the sailors freedom. I wanted the life that they had. The large looming ships and the impressive timber masts had me in awe, and when I would sit with the sailors and the other freight haulers in the dockside bars enraptured by their stories of the seas, I would cringe inside at my own inferiority in their presence.

The dockside work was dreary. It rained almost everyday and I was nowhere near as well equipped as the other men. A lot of us workers though were in similar situations. We were boys no older than twenty or so. I was lucky that I was fairly tall and broad for my age as it made the work fairly easy for me. I have to admit that I fell into some bad company while I worked on the docksides. There were a lot of misfits that were part of our group, and though I wasn't green around the gills like some of the boys, I found them to be fearful and a lot of the time they would easily be able to pressure me into one thing or another without my say so. And I played along just so that I could fit in with them and would not be a target for their ire or humility. Out of all of them that was one person who I really felt I could trust. Trust is a loosely used word here, for boys or young men such as myself in those times, determining who was trustworthy and who was not, was not something that could easily be established.

On the outside people have many layers. I told no one where I had truly come from or who I was, for awhile I even used a fake name; but I quickly gave that up once I let it slip. I quickly became friends with a man a few years older than me; his name was Joshua and he had been working on the dockside for a year before I had got there. He had a smarmy, clever sort of personality but I couldn't notice the disingenuous smile constantly plastered across his face. For a long while I shared a living space with him. Joshua had a room on the dockside that was large enough for me to sleep on a pile of blankets on the floor, and in return he was kind enough to alleviate me of ¾ of my pay in return for shelter, I did not complain though. This was the first time that I was truly working for myself, I was no burden on my father or mother, and so I was more than satisfied with having a relatively safe and comfortable place to sleep, a friend and my own money. I wasn't by far Joshua's closest friend, as I say he had such an enigmatic personality – plenty of people felt they were probably his best friend.

My life likely would not have turned out as it had if I had never met Joshua. If Joshua had not left. Saying *left* is simplifying the fact that he was killed. There was never an official investigation in his murder. Joshua was a migrant that was in the country without naturalisation papers or any papers of the kind, and so the police were largely unbothered by his demise.

I remember it was a very bright day in the middle of summer when it happened. It was hot and muggy, and though we were along the waterfront, the close proximity to the water made little to no difference to the sweat that was pouring off of our bodies. I don't know exactly what happened, but Joshua and another man – I forget his name now – but I remember he was a big brute of a man with a face like a squashed potato and a frown to go along with it. The two of them had gotten into some sort of argument, that was likely over a girl, some money or a job – we tended to argue about almost everything and anything back then. However, this argument had begun to look as if it would come to blows and a lot of the men had stopped working to watch, and a few others had made their way over to the two, to try and separate them. No one wanted to be punished for not working hard enough, and the huge size of Joshua's adversary, made me fear for my friend, though I could get no closer to him due to the other men that were in my way.

I could only watch from a distance as the altercation happened however, it was broken up by the taskmaster and the two of them were separated as far away as they possibly could get from each other. Later on, as we were finishing up work, Joshua, myself and some of the other boys were making our way too get drinks. It was then that I asked him what the altercation was about. Joshua sneered, the unpleasant smile never really leaving his face even when he was disgusted, and his lips turned down. He seemed to be lost in the memory for the moment, and we all looked with bated breath as we walked along, waiting for what he would say. However, just as he was able to tell us what happened a large, fast-moving shadow stepped out quickly from the alleyway and before any of us could react, the shadow barrelled straight into Joshua. Both he and the shadow, which we now saw to be his adversary from earlier, crashed onto the floor in a large and loud tumble. I remember I could hear growling from the man, it was quite clearly the man whom Joshua had argued with, but he was growling like some sort of animal. From where I was stood to the side, I could only see him in profile but I could see his large moustachioed face growling with anger as he glared down into Joshua's surprised, and no longer sneering face. Joshua's shocked face remained that way, as his head was knocked once into the stone ground, and it took a moment for us bystanders also to realise exactly what happened. The slowly widening black-red pool of blood around his head like a macabre halo though, was more than enough to alert us that Joshua was truly dead. His eyes bulged grotesquely out of his face in a shocked death-mask and his mouth stood open.

It was quiet then. We were along the side of the wharf where there were not many people at this time of night. As we tended to finish working late, there were only a select number of drinking establishments that opened late so they could receive us as customers – we did after all tend to spend quite a bit of money drinking well into the night. This meant however, that despite dockworkers, there were not many people around. In the immediate vicinity; there were the four of us that had been walking with Joshua, Joshua himself and the attacker, who was crouched over him like some sort of snarling beast.

For a moment it was dead quiet. We could hear the laboured breathing of the brute, but nobody moved, and nobody said anything. I don't know if it was fear of the man that stopped any of us from speaking but we just watching until he rose staggering drunkenly, and without looking back stepped over the pool of congealing black around Joshua's head and continued walking. I watched him until he was entirely out of sight, his staggering, lumbering gait disappearing into the darkness. It was only then that I noticed that the other men had crouched down beside Joshua. His death was quite apparent and we all looked at each other unsure of exactly what we were supposed to do in this circumstance. Mike seemed to be the only one with any sense in that moment, and he stood. He managed to convince us that we needed to leave – and so we did. We split. All of us trying to not look suspicious. We all went off home. We saw each other again the next day on the quayside, and through some unspoken agreement acted as though nothing had happened. The taskmaster asked where Joshua was, but we all claimed we did not know, kept our heads down and continued to work. His assailant said nothing obviously. The taskmaster did come up to me though, asking me specifically where Joshua was seeing as I shared a room with him, and surely I should know where he was. I told him I did not and I had not seen him since we left work the day before.

Joshua's death was the first true loss I had encountered in my life. I don't count the loss of my parents as a loss. They did not want me and I too, to some extent, did not want them. But Joshua was different – he had been like a brother, father and mother all at once at times.

After that life continued on as normal. I got into a relationship of sorts with a girl that I knew. She was easy to impress and I liked that about her – it made her interesting unlike the boring stuffy girls that I knew growing up. Eliza was her name. She was so pretty even when she was a roaring drunk, and often fawned over other men through her job. She was nice, and though I don't think I was especially attracted to her, there was something about her that made me want to be around her often. I think she felt the same with me. She always spent a great deal of time with me and stopped others from taking too much issue with me. Eliza was like a big sister to me and I loved her and I knew she loved me also as a little brother.

After Joshua's death I couldn't afford the room any more; even though he was no longer taking my wages. It was so that I moved into the brothel in which Eliza worked nightly. I had been there before to see her and all the women there were all very nice to me. They treated me like a little brother – even though some of them were a lot younger than I was. It was a nice and comfortable place to live and of course I got plenty of snide comments from my work fellows, who in no uncertain terms jeered at me and claimed that I must have been a whore myself for living in a whorehouse, but I ignored them. And of course I also got a lot of teasing from those who thought that I must get a lot of discounts. I did not, and I wasn't interested in the women in that way. The women looked after me there, and for the first time in my life I felt looked after.

I lived there for four years with Eliza and the women. They fed me, gave me a room to myself, and let me work in the brothel as a kind of security. I quit my job on the dockside and worked as a chaperone, security guard and a concierge for the owner of the brothel; Madame Profonde.

Madame Profonde liked me also. She let me help her with all sorts of tasks and whenever there was a need for a man to be present for some dealing or another, that were mostly illegal or illicit, I was able to help her out. I think she saw me as an impromptu grandson, having no children of her own. I liked that about Madame Profonde – that she saw me as a stroke of luck to end up living there. I knew a lot of the patrons and no one tended to take much of an issue with me and I was glad of that. Madame Profonde hired other security also, despite many of the girls being more than capable to hold their own in the face of aggression. I was more of a safety net to prevent fights in the establishment and to deal with the more rowdy customers. I was happy to be there, and I was happy that they were happy I was there.

When I was in my mid twenties I was working at the brothel full time. It was during my second year of working there that I had an altercation that was to change my life irreparably. It was a usual night; the girls were all busy running around as we had a show on that night which made especially busy. This meant I had more work to do securing the building, and though I was working with other security guards, I was the main concierge.

Eliza had quite a few customers that night that I already knew of, and there were always patrons that walked in when they pleased. That night though there was a man who disturbed me as soon as I caught sight of him. He was quite short and walked with a sailor's gait, and he swayed as he waltzed drunkenly down the dimly lit corridors of the brothel. He had a large, thick black beard that shrouded his face and beady grey eyes. His skin was a pallid white and his hair, what meagre amount there was of it, hung limply down the back of his head. He looked untrustworthy, and Madame Profonde and I had a silent agreement too watch the man. The other security were also informed.

Though his appearance was very fitting to the bad feeling he gave off, he was unfortunately one of Eliza's clients, and though I tried to plead with her to not take him in, she ignored me, as she stated that the opportunity to turn down a paying customer was ludicrous. All I could do then was just stand back and wait.

I waited outside Eliza's room that night. This was not uncommon behaviour for me. Occasionally I would stand outside of Eliza's room, a protective brotherly instinct in me causing me to wait and make sure that Eliza was okay after the clients left. That night the raucous of the show that was in full swing on the floor below permeating through the floorboards and onto the first floor where I was stood. I tried to block out the sounds that I could always hear when Eliza was working, and had got rather good at it. I was sort of immune to it now though it disturbed me at first, and for a long time I would wait on the stairs instead, but slowly I became used to the sounds and they became background noise to me. All of the girls rooms were the same – I could pretty much hear everything, and because there were gaps under the door, lights from inside the rooms could be seen from the corridor.

It was known that the girls kept their lights on and if there was a problem they would blow out the candles. That night however, Lisa did not get the chance to blow out the candles. I was resting against the wall staring into nothing when I heard a loud thump, a cry that sounded very much like Eliza and a grunt from the man. Initially I did not want to enter. It was not unknown that some of the men used violence in their exchanges, and a lot of them paid a lot more for it, but I knew Eliza did not accept these clients and so I became concerned.

I took a step closer to the door when another thump resounded, I called out softly to Eliza. I heard no response, but yet another cry wailed out. As I stepped closer still, my hand reaching for the doorknob, the door was slammed open and hit the wall inside the room. The short gruff man from earlier barged past me, knocking into my shoulder as he spat something back at me and continued his ambling march down the corridor, grumbling the whole way. I looked after him for a moment and saw him go down the stairs where there was more security and more people. I did not feel like he would cause that much of a problem and if he did there would be people to sort it, so I rushed into Eliza's room and found her slumped against her bed. I looked around hastily for blood and found nothing. As I checked her over though, I noticed that Eliza's face cheek was deeply reddened and I assumed the man had hit her.

I begged Eliza to tell me what had happened, but she would not until I threatened to tell Madame Profonde. She then told me that the man was a debt collector for her brother who owed certain large debts. The man was there to take it from her as her brother had said that she was the one that would be able to pay. I knew that was not true of course, as most of the girl's money went to Madame Profonde and they only kept a small amount for themselves. The man's audacity angered me, and I marched after him with Eliza calling at the back of me to wait. I ignored her and shot down the stairs searching the crowd that was gathered around the show, trying not to cause too much attention to myself should Madame Profonde become aware of me. I saw the man downing a glass of something in the corner. The audacity that he had to wait around after hitting Eliza infuriated me, and I marched across the room. He looked up rather late, his eyes unfocused but he moved in enough time to make a

174

scramble for the door as he saw me descending upon him.

It occurred to me only afterward that I most likely cut quite an imposing figure. I was a tall man and largely built, and was stalking towards a drunk man who had just hit someone dear to me. He managed to get out the door before I got to him; which I was glad of, as I did not want Madame Profonde or anyone else to witness what would happen next. He got a few paces away from the front door before I dragged him by the top of his arm, probably too tightly by the way that he strained against me, and into an unlit alleyway.

I pushed him against the wall and demanded to know why he had hit Eliza. He sneered at me in his drunken way, his reeking breath made my eyes water but I pushed on, still digging his shoulders into the rough brick. I remember the look of that man. Drunk out of his mind as he stumbled over his explanation for hitting Eliza. I forget exactly what he said to me, probably some nonsense, and I don't remember exactly what it was that caused me to snap and punch him right in the same cheek that he had struck Eliza.

175

He fell to the floor as the impact of my fist sent him down onto his knees. I kicked him then. And I kept punching and kicking him until his face was a bloody mess, his eyes puffed up, his nose broken in more than one place and his lips busted beyond use. He was curled up in a miserable ball on the ground at my feet. The commotion had attracted any attention at all. It was loud in the brothel, and it was loud on the street and where we were was entirely unlit – I only knew where he was through the sounds he made. His drunkenness made it impossible for him to fight back against me, and I was glad of that.

After I had calmed myself somewhat, my fists caked with blood and probably cut themselves with the way that they were stinging, I looked down at the man. He was still. I thought I had killed him. I rubbed by bloodied fists off on his dirty jacket and I marched out of the alleyway in the opposite direction of the brothel.

I kept walking for a long time, hours perhaps, and by the time I returned to the brothel door some hours later, the sky was lightening. The streets were quiet. All the patrons had gone home, the girls were asleep and Madame Profonde was most likely asleep also. I let myself in and made my way tiredly up the stairs, my cracked knuckles congealed with blood. I fell into my bed and drifted quickly into a thick and heavy sleep.

The next day Eliza gave me a discreet though disappointed but slightly appreciative look when she saw my knuckles. Madame Profonde pretended not to notice, and some of the other girls made jokes, but nobody really wanted to know – Eliza being the only one who knew first hand. I think she was thankful but also quite disappointed in my violence, I gave her no details though and she asked for none.

I went out late in the afternoon as I had slept in quite late, and the brothel did not open until later that evening – after the previous night's show the girls were all tired, and so I decided to go out for a walk. There was some groceries that Madame Profonde wanted me to purchase, but after the debacle the night before I needed to refresh myself. To pretend that my knuckles weren't cracked with large cuts, that had digged into the flesh of that sweaty little man.

I was ambling along the quayside staring out at the water and watching the passers-by when he came towards me. The same man from the night before. He was swaying tipsily towards me, and I found I was both surprised and relieved that I hadn't killed him. It was miraculous that he was up and about walking – though with quite a considerable limp, and his face a disgusting mess of bruised flesh. In fact he looked rather more dead than alive, but he was quite clearly drunk again. I considered turning around and walking the other way should he recognise me. Instead I put my head down and kept walking, I intended to pretend that I did not know him.

When he was around a foot away from me, I looked up at the man. His eyes were not focused – just as they had been the night before. He did not look at me, and he kept walking his limping, drunken seaman's swagger. He did not recognise me and I had got away with what I had done. Of course I did not though. It is never that simple, is it?

A few months later, when I had thought the incident entirely behind me, I was confronted one evening as I was on my way home, by three men I did not recognise, though they seemed to recognise me quite clearly. They addressed me quite unashamedly as 'the man-whore that works in the brothel', and proceeded to inflict upon me the same wounds that I had inflicted upon the disgusting man that had harmed Eliza.

They broke one of my legs, gave me two black-eyes and left me for dead; just as I left the Eliza's attacker. It is a cyclical world that we live in, and I felt no grief in my wounds. They were well deserved I thought for a defending Eliza. That was the second time my life changed irreparably. I was brought back to the brothel by two sailors who found me a few hours later. Madame Profonde was beside herself. She would not look me in the eye. and it was one of the girls who informed me that Eliza was dead. She had been stabbed in her bed by a client who nobody could properly identify except from the fact that he had red hair. He came and went quickly they said, and nobody could find him since most likely he had hopped on the next ship out of the country.

I was distraught. The pain from my leg was irradiating through my whole body, and the pain from Eliza's death was overwhelming. Madame Profonde seemed to think it was my fault and as promptly as she did everything, she cast me out on the street. This too, I suppose I had coming. I had no belongings to really speak of – my diary was in my jacket pocket and was thrown after me. My leg had been roughly set by the sailors, Madame Profonde had allowed this at least before pushing me out onto the street with an old umbrella but I was to use as a crutch.

I had never lived on the streets before and really I suppose I did not after being thrown out. I had a taste of it for about 2 hours, slumped in the corner of the alleyway that I had almost half killed that horrible man, when the stark afternoon sunlight was overshadowed by a figure. I groaned slightly, thinking that it would be the men from earlier come back to finish the job as they had done with Eliza, when the shadow stretched out its hand and asked me in a very smooth and quite beautiful voice if I needed somewhere to stay. The sun entirely blocked out the features of the man. He was just a looming shadow and a voice, that stood over me. I squinted up at him.

I knew I did not look homeless at that point, though the splint that was connected to my leg had caused my trousers to be roughly cut. It was probably obvious then, that I was in no good shape. Did this man go around picking up strangers daily? He seemed odd and untrustworthy, and I grunted as a means to wave him off. I turned my head back down to stare into my lap, when I heard a snort from above me before the figure crouched down so that he was eye level with me.

He had a disarming and pleasant smile on his face. And his large green-brown eyes stood out against his warm skin. He was dressed well and asked his question again, this time assuring me that he had a spare room that I could take and that he was looking for some labour. I was not stupid, and no pleasing smile would make me go follow a complete stranger. But something about the man made me believe that he was telling the truth. He laughed again at my scrutinising look, and offered instead to buy me a meal and something to drink, and if I then felt up to it there was a top floor room that he admitted was nothing more than a cupboard but was free for me to take. If I went with him, I could then decide afterward if I wished to work with him or not.

My stomach whined at the prospect of food, and I truly did not want to be on the streets when night came. For how long would I be in this position? The dockyards always needed hands, but my association with Joshua and my initial leaving to work for Madame Profonde was well known. I weighed up my options, which were admittedly not great, and took a leap of faith and replied to the man that food was an accepted start. He grinned again, and showing considerable strength, pulled me up by my arm, and waited for me to settle standing with my broke leg. He then cut a brisk pace out of the alley and into the street proper, I having no choice but to follow this enigmatic stranger.

Chapter 6

Blue

His name was Mr Ferguson and he lived in a modestly sized house in the city proper. It was a brightly-lit two storey house; the kind that has a large staircase that led up to the front door. The house inside of the house was richly decorated, with a wide range of top of the range furnishings but what I thought was the most beautiful was the lightly coloured and expensive wallpaper on the hall walls that were unlike anything I had seen before. My eyes traced the intricate designs on the walls every time I walked past them. There was also a spacious receiving room and living room as well as a lavishly decorated dinning room. I couldn't help but notice that the house was so beautifully decorated and housed people that were so vastly different from me socially and financially, and that I in some way tainted the atmosphere in there and immediately felt self-conscious stood in the entry way. Mr Ferguson however, seemed oblivious to my inner strife and sauntered around his home showing me where everything was, much in the same way he had strode up to me in the alleyway.

Charles Ferguson was around my age, perhaps a year or two older, and though I never asked, I took him to be around 26 or 27. He had tightly coiled black hair that sat just above his nape in the style that was extremely fashionable and I was entirely envious of. I always thought he was a rather regal man – a prince in plain-clothes. When he paid for the supper as he had promised, I couldn't hep but feel inferior to him we sat across from each other. My clothes were by no means dirty, but they were obviously cheaper and more worn-out than Charles well tailored suit and coat. The entire walk over to the house, Charles chattered on, and I who was sullen and largely silent, grunted only when necessary. I felt somewhat like I was walking to the end of *something*. It was bad enough that my life had got the point that I was following stranger home in search of some stability for my own. I resented the part of me that did not have the guts to stow away on some vessel and never look back.

Charles did not live alone. He and his sister Esther had lived together after their father, who had been looking after them, had died suddenly. Their mother had never really been in the picture as she had died when Esther was small, and so they had been raised solely by their father. The fresh grief from the death of her father, was obvious on Esther's face. I hesitated to ask when their father had died, but it was clear that it had been recently, perhaps within the past few years.

Mr Charles Ferguson, whose home I stepped into however, was a counterfeiter – I'm sure much to the chagrin of his deceased, but once lawyer, father. Charles made a comfortable sum selling altered and also creating intricate official papers, and he in turn was able to send Esther to a well-to-do college for girls. She was studying languages, and I often heard her practising, her divinely melodic voice, snippets of German or French in her room.

I found out Charles' profession early on. Oddly enough he seemed to have no reservations in telling me – a complete stranger who for all he knew would report him to the police. When I mentioned this to him however, he threw his head back and laughed rather uproariously, claiming that I looked more like the type that would see what I could get out of a deal such as this, rather than rat him out.

He wasn't wrong. I had known more unsavoury types than a middle-class young counterfeiter. And my young mind thought the whole thing rather intriguing anyway and had no qualms with Charles' job. I admit that the business intrigued me and I quickly took up his offer of lodging and subsequently became employed through him as a sort of runner for him; fetching materials and the like from suppliers. At first he did not entrusted me with delivering his creations, and a lot of the time his clients would come to the house to receive their goods anyway. He did allow me to be present at some of these meetings occasionally, and it was a thrill to be a part of it.

Truly, I think he more included me there as a subtle security; not dissimilar to my time at Madam Profonde's. I did not mind though, it was a way to make money and I was saving the small amount I earned under the mattress in my room – I planned to leave as soon as I

186

had enough money to book passage for across the Chanel. I had a plan back then to travel to France, start again there and actually build a proper life for myself from the roots. I was still young and good, sturdy hands were always in demand everywhere. I was grateful for Charles' hospitality, but I wanted to stand alone for a change. And that's what I was aiming for.

Another perk of living with Mr Grayson, was Esther. Esther was a lovely girl a few years younger than myself, and I almost never saw her as she attended the girls college most days and was never permitted to be visible in the house when clients arrived (for her own safety so Charles said). Her timidity and apprehension of me thoroughly interested me, and I found myself following her around a room with my eyes. I tried to be subtle but I think she caught on. Charles had no idea. She spent much of her time in her room though, and only ventured out in the evenings to cook and keep house; these being the only times I was privy to her delicate face. Esther always wore her dark hair down her back, the thick and compact glossy coils hanging loosely with the top of her hair twisted up into artful braids around her crown. Her skin was a deeper, warmer tone than her brother's, by only a fraction. It was likely that no one was likely to notice such a thing, but I spent so much time looking at her from a far. I committed every glimpse and glance of her that I could to my memory.

She disliked me at first I think. In her defence I did not blame her. I was a strange man in her house. And when I observed her interactions with her brother, it was obvious to see that they were close and was I then some sort of threat to her brother's attention? Over time though she realised that I had no intention of getting between them and she warmed to me fractionally. Though I still had to trail behind her brother every working day and then even on some days off, I spent all the free time I had tuning my entire being to Esther.

I couldn't rightly say what it was about her that I found so intriguing, but I new that I had never felt this way about a girl before. When I first moved to the dockside, I was too young to really appreciate them. When working at Madam Profonde's, girls and women became something for me to protect and equally be protected by, not something for me to desire. People in general did not really interest me all that much either sexually nor romantically, and this was the first time at the ripe age of 24, that someone did. Almost everything I did was in some way linked to Esther, and if it wasn't my mind would be wondering back to her regardless.

One afternoon, I was returning home through the markets stalls after purchasing a specific paper type that Charles requested. With the sheaves tucked securely under my arm and my hands pushed delinquently into my trouser pockets I leisurely perused the stalls, taking in the bustling atmosphere that made up the markets. It was a fairly hot day in June, and the sky was entirely cloudless – allowing the full intensity of the early summer sun to pierce through the vast blue and force patches of sweat to collect under my armpits and down my back. I had long stopped wearing my jacket out since the weather improved a week or so ago and was in that moment, glad of it. The markets were doubly hot from the teeming crowds that trudged through them. It was interesting in the inner city, and different from the docks in a multitude of ways. There was such a mix of people and groups and everyone person was so different in class, race or creed to the next, it was impossible to feel out of place. There were always food vendors out at these markets and their wares mixed together in the air and created an almost putrid amalgamation of scents that offended anyone visiting for the first time. Newcomers were fairly easy to spot with their handkerchiefs pressed firmly against their noses.

What was especially nice about the markets was the mix of goods on offer. There were various local goods besides food that included; cloth, ready made clothing, boot sellers, delicate ceramics, currency exchangers, book sellers, sellers of rare goods and toy merchants. As well as foreign goods such as spices and silks, there were marvellously moustachioed sellers that brandished glimmering bronze wares and small wooden or jade figures. There was a wide assortment of knick knacks and curios that shone in the sunlight and caught my eye, even though I had seen them day after day.

I never bought anything from these merchants, preferring to buy fruit to eat on the way home from whatever errand Charles had sent me on. But that day I stopped in front of a silk merchant. I knew that silk was not a material I could afford. But above this stall and on a low table amongst the large rolls of the fabric, was an assortment of thin strips of silk that where about half a metre long and some smaller pieces that looked to be around an arms length. The fabric was sheered into thin strips intending to be ribbons. They came in a dazzling assortment of bright crimsons, rich ambers, startling emeralds and profound maroons. What particularly caught my eye though, was the deepest ocean-blue ribbon I had ever seen. It looked so vibrant and ethereal as it fluttered in the slight twinkle of wind along the wrong rod that they were lain across. The other colours seemed to diminish in beauty in the presence of it.

There was one person only that I thought of in that moment that to me, made all other beauty seen insignificant. I had the most vivid impression of that blue ribbon fluttering in Esther's hair, tied up into her plaits and trailing down her back in the most lovely way.

I waited until the attention of the merchant was busy, he was extorting an out-of-towner with a ludicrous price for a bolt of purple silk. I knew the ribbon would cost my entire wage that I had only been paid this morning, and so buying it was entirely out the question. Truthfully, I don't think I had any true intention of actually purchasing it. I was saving a majority of my wage for my boat ticket, but in that moment, I new also that I had to have that ribbon. With no preamble I slipped the small piece of silk into my hand as I walked through the market, the fabric securely bundled in my trouser pocket as I headed home.

When I arrived home that afternoon, the delicate silk of the ribbon caressed my hand as I placed my hand in my trouser pocket to retrieve my key.

••••

That night I lost an opportunity. It was a usual night where Charles and I sat around the table as Esther served us dinner. The ribbon burned a hole in my pocket yet still I did not present it to her, not being able to find a time there and then with Charles present. I did not give her the ribbon that night or the day afterwards either, for that night I came down with a horrendous bout of the flu and was bedridden for days. Charles was the one that nursed me between his own work, Esther busy with her school work. I was delirious for most of my illness and I feared that in my delirium that I would say something to Charles about my feelings for Esther.

I remember a state of blurry consciousness during the worst of the illness when the closeness of the walls felt suffocating. They were painted white but had been sun-bleached into a light cream over the years. I remember that they seemed to swirl and pulsate like a large canvas of flesh. I had to toss and turn to try and getaway from it as it tried to press down on me from all sides. There was a peculiar smell that I remembered as I lay in that bed as the walls suffocating me. It was a smell that I couldn't quite place. It was cloying and choking – the smell of being unable to breathe or talk. I never knew at the time how long these delusions would last in reality, but I would be conscious to the changes in light to the drastic black pitch of the middle of the night when I would awake alone, covered in sweat as the pulsating walls receded and instead the inky blackness suffocated me in its place. In the morning my mind was assaulted with the contrast of the startling and horrific white yellow of the sunlight, that filtered through the open windows that Charles kept open. I remember in small moments of lucidity that I couldn't feel the breeze. It scared me I knew that the wind was blowing I could see the curtains move but I couldn't feel it on my skin that was burning hotter than ever. I feared that wind would carry me off and away and I would be unable to stop it.

Out of all of it I suppose I remember Charles; not that I had a concrete image of him in my mind, as I was so delirious. I remember the soft pressure of a damp cloth on my forehead and I remember the soothing touch on my arm every now, I remember him being there in the room with me even though I couldn't really make him out during the height of the fever. The fever broke in the middle of the night on the fourth day. I found out later that a doctor had been called out twice to check on me, as the fever did not seem to want to want break.

When I woke it was quiet. Too quiet. I guessed it to be around two or three o'clock in the morning. I could hear a distant shout of a reveller from somewhere across town, but that was really it – there's nothing to be heard that early in the morning. The house was unusually quiet also, not even the periodic groaning of the eaves could be heard.

 I lay awake and a great deal less sweaty than when I had woken up previously, but my nightshirt clung to my chest and back in a disagreeable damp. My eyes were barely focused as I tracked the shadows around my room. The window was still open I noticed then, but I think what really made me understand that my fever had broken is that I could actually feel the breeze. It was caressing and light, it felt like the soothing touch someone or something.

I don't know how long I lay there. My head had a strange feeling that was not quite pain but muffled cloudiness. Despite this I felt marginally well. I had felt so ill the past few days and when I felt lucid enough to actually *feel* something during my illness – it was just felt numbness. However, there was something other than clarity that I felt when I woke in that house. I had been living there for only two months but I felt a sense of belonging, something that I had never felt with my parents who had always handled me as a burden on them. That was until I met Joshua and I felt like I had a brother with him, the same feeling of belonging could be said for my time with Madame Profonde and the girls – but not in the same intensity as the connection I felt with Charles and Esther. I felt again like I was something just to be used something that was convenient, but here with Charles and Esther I felt like I was a long lost sibling or cousin. I felt like I had a purpose but whatever that was, it was hidden from me in that moment, but I felt severity of it in my fate.

My relationship with Charles had improved greatly. I think he caught on that I quite liked Esther. He had not said anything of it of course, but I think he probably would not have complained if we should have married. We were still very young of course and I had no intention of marrying Esther right then, and I don't think she had any intention of marrying me. I still had a lot to figure out for myself as it was and I quite liked living there sort of like Charles' younger brother.

What I did not want was for Charles to not see me as someone worthy to have in his life. I loved Esther, but the way that I loved Charles also was very important to me. But he also seemed like a gatekeeper to the things that I wanted. He stood in the way of me and Esther. I did not resent him for that though. Not in the way I had resented my father.

Once I had got a lot better I went out again running errands for Charles, and I had entirely forgotten about the ribbon until I saw Esther one morning – she looked as lovely as she usually did with her hair fully plaited and coiled up on top of her head. That day I slipped my hand into my pocket and thought of the ribbon for the first time, it felt, in ages. Charles thankfully was not around as He did gone out to meet a client.

I think I startled Esther as I stood there at the threshold of the kitchen watching her as she prepared lunch for the day. My hand was clenched in my pocket and I'm sure I looking more like a bewildered animal than a man about to give a gift to a woman. However, I *did* present to the ribbon in a rather ungainly and awkward flourish. I clutched the soft fabric in my fist; the delicacy of the ribbon as it dangled down between my fingers was a stark contrast to the aggressive thrust of my fist in the air.

For a moment Esther just stared at me and her all fairness I did look odd as I stood there rather awkwardly with one hand clutched at my side and the other thrust forward dangling a blue ribbon in front of her. I stammered out why I bought it for her, obviously she did not need to know that I had pilfered it. For a terrifying moment she said nothing and blankly stared at me as she flicked her eyes intermittently between me and the ribbon. The silence and uneasiness lasted so long that I thought she would not take it, and I started to feel rather embarrassed, after all why would someone as delicate and as successful as Esther have any interest in a hulking mess like me? However, my self-depreciation was uncalled for as she smiled, a rather private smile, and

198

stepped forward lightly as she delicately pulled the ribbon from my clenched fist. She thanked me in the most delicate and innocent way before pulling a single pin out of her hair – letting down the coil of plaits that she had tied her hair into in a few swift movements. Gracefully she tied the ribbon delicately into a small bow at the base of her neck, bunching together her braids into a bouquet here. I immediately thought that forget-me-nots would look absolutely delightful in the deep brown of her hair. I was truly happy that she liked my gift, and I stood there for a moment smiling like a buffoon before she stepped forward again on light feet and gave me the lightest kiss on my cheek. She took an amused second to study me before she turned into the kitchen again. I was dumbfounded and I had no idea what to do next. On halted steps I simply turned away and headed back up the stairs to my attic room.

I decided that night to celebrate Esther was staying overnight at her school dormitory that night and Charles retired early to work on a document for a new customer, the details of which I was not privy to. So I decided to go out. Going out was not something I did occasionally or very often actually I preferred to stay inside with Charles and Esther; talk to them, drink with Charles or eat and talk to Esther about what she was doing at school. I haven't been out drinking since Joshua. So it was a rather novel experience for me especially after being forced out of Madame Profonde's.

This was why I was forced to wonder aimlessly for a while a long the dockside before I came to a pub I had never been in before. Despite having no actual qualms with any of the men in that pub who were all strangers, I managed to generate enough animosity and within 20 minutes of sitting down for a drink I had a new black eye. I wasn't going to fight anyone however and so I braced myself on the floor in which I had been dispatched, anticipating a second punch to the face. It did not come however, just as that early afternoon in the alleyway, Charles was bent over me slightly his shadow obscuring the light that hung from the ceiling. He did not look upset or disappointed in me but there was concern it on his face, and at a questioning glance, the man who had caused argument with me seemed to be seem to have been removed from the building, I'm not sure if that was due to Charles' presence or the bartender's actions. Regardless I was elated that no fight had occurred.

I remember Charles dragging me up by the arm and my wincing being ignored by him as he dragged me through the door of the bar. He walked back home at a rather brisk pace, all the while explaining to me that he had been walking past that bar on his way out to visit a client, when he saw the altercation. He saw me being hit down through the open door and he offered to pay off the man to leave there and then. Though he had missed his meeting with his client he seemed unconcerned, stating that the client would understand and that a little mystery never harmed meeting.

He was silent then. When we were only about 10 minutes or so away from the house Charles stopped and turned to me – the amber of the street lamps flickered in the light hazel flecks of his eyes. I thought that in that moment he looked more regal than ever. And it shocked me how similar Esther and Charles were; almost as though they could have been twins despite the age difference.

I stopped when he did and turned to look at him. The shallow wound on my head was bleeding profusely and dripping onto my shirt- the stream made worse through the tears that I had to keep blinking back as the blood dripped in my eye. I tried to focus on Charles as my head pounded and lights danced in front of my eyes. He did not try to aid me and I did not want him to it. Strangely, it was then that he offered me a position of being his true assistant. He would need to teach me some simple crafts and proper counterfeiting, but after four or five years I could be a partner of his. Though I thought his timing to bring up this conversion was strange, I readily agreed. It was an opportunity of stability, and I could stay close to Esther. I could marry her – if I was his partner he would never say no to a marriage between us. I shook his hand with so much enthusiasm that Charles broke into and easy and hearty laugh that I don't think I had ever heard from him, and we continued on our way back home.

••••

For the next few years I worked hard everyday. I was working with Charles to make perfect counterfeit copies. It seemed that there was someone who always wanted to scam someone else. I had started off with the basics by forging lettering and then Charles had me working on four pieces on my own. He still led most of the meetings with clients but now I could go along with him to them and stand beside him and make comments if need be, though hardly ever offers of my own.

Charles seemed happy with me and *I* was happy with me also. I was finally getting a better chance at life than I had originally been given and I felt more and more pleased with myself everyday. I was 24 at this point and Charles had grow into comfortable bachelor. It surprised me offer than he had not caught any of the eyes of any of the ladies that were around. I did not question about it rather wanting to keep him and Esther to myself anyway. Esther had grown so lovely in those two years. To the point that one day as Charles and I were working I couldn't help but ask him if it was possible for me to marry Esther when she became say 22. Charles did not look up from his work, and the response I got was am undignified snort. Apparently it had taken me a year longer than he had thought I would to ask. I couldn't help but laugh also ha. I was happy that he was willing to accept me as a brother in law.

At that time I would have done anything for Esther, she was the most important thing to me. I had long given up my dream of crossing the channel along time ago, perhaps as soon as she is accepted my ribbon, from that moment I decided to devote my every waking moment to her. I could tell it wasn't one sided either, she was clearly very interested in me also. Despite the fact that I had Charles' assent he never seemed ready to make it official. He would often drag the issue out and state that the time would come when it came. Always stating that at the moment we had too many clients to deal with and were far too busy to think of weddings. I always half-heartedly agreed as I did not want to get on Charles' bad side, but he was so blasé about the issue that it began to grate on my nerves.

In April it was Esther's birthday, and as a gift I procured her a sapphire brooch. It was wrought in silver to look like a flower with a cluster of small sapphires encased in the middle.

It would have cost me two months worth of rent.

It was such a beautiful piece – the stones were minute to the point you could hardly even see them but they were so vibrant in colour and they complimented Esther so wonderfully. If the delightful squeal she gave out was anything to go by, she also liked them, and Charles' approving smile gave me further pride.

Esther's birthday was a wonderful affair. Charles had paid for Esther to get a professional photo taken by a French photographer who was extremely popular with the middling and upper middling sorts that Charles was acquainted with in his business. Charles enjoyed the benefits of these connections by getting a substantial discount from the photographer, and as Esther was sat perched on the divan ready to have her photo taken, I

205

couldn't help but feel as though my life was going by too quickly. My life was so perfect and I was running out of time.

It was decided that the photo would be placed upon the mantel next to the painting of their father, who had been sternly surveying the sitting room for years. The portrait disturbed me and I tried not to go in there alone. His large whiskers were intimidating as he looked down on me with his lone monocle. I   remember Esther telling me that he was blind in one eye. She said it always used to scare her when she was little, now she though whenever she saw a man with one blind eye, it always reminded her her father. The photo of Esther was very beautiful and Esther never looked more pretty. The black and white tone of the photograph made it so that you couldn't see the colour of her brooch, but it was there in the picture. And everybody that lived in that house knew who had gifted it to her. I loved that picture and it made me want to go into the sitting room and defy her dead fathers gaze, to take in the preserved beauty of the daughter. The father was not around, I had only to

206

contend with the approval the brother. I made no attempt, as some would have, to go to find wherever the elder Mr Grayson was laid to rest. I did not want approval from the dead.

That night, when Esther was tucked quietly into her bed, Charles and I sat down in the sitting room; the low light from the fireplace was burning quietly with coals and gave a soft hue to the room. We had a single lamp on also that broke up the dark slightly. Charles and I were both reclined in deep, plush couches enjoying the evening. We often had quiet drinks into the evening after we had finished our work as a sort of celebration for all of the hard work we had put in during the day. That day it felt doubly celebratory with Esther's birthday that had gone so well. She had seemed so happy and that was something that both Charles and I were always looking for – Esther's happiness.

It often surprised me how much I was invested in Esther's happiness, as though I had known her all my life; that was how deep my love for her extended. A small hopeful and desperate part of me hoped that

Charles would perhaps bring up the idea of marriage at that point – he did not and I sort of resented him a little bit despite his long and murmuring speech on how he was happy to have me as part of his family. This filled me with quite a lot of joy and I was extremely happy that Charles accepted me. That was after all what I wanted – to be a part of his family. To be with him and Esther. His hesitation in making me his brother-in-law though rankled me, and in that moment I rather hated him. The dying coals in the fireplace were a deep contrast to the fizzling anger and frustration that was building up inside of my own chest.

Chapter 7
Spray

The next five years passed very quickly and my relationship with Charles and Esther improved. Esther and I grew closer, though I felt frustrated that our relationship was less romantic and more like that of siblings. With Charles though, I felt that the two of us had become closer than ever. He seemed to have warmed-up to me and I couldn't help but be intrigued by him, not only as a patron and a business partner but in a more intimate sense – as a member of his family. Despite the half year that I had stayed with them, I had never heard any mention of any other family from them; other than that stern painting of their father that stood his serious vigil above the mantle in the front room. They seemed to be alone in the world – a small island unto themselves in which I had shipwrecked and upended the intricacy of their existence in such a short amount of time. Despite this, neither they nor in fact myself, saw any occasion to change or current status quo, despite the apparent strangeness of it to outsiders. We had, in the past, been asked inquiring questions by curious or just plain nosey customers or acquaintances about the nature of my appearance and role in their lives, which neither myself nor Charles saw fit to give details for. Further, the business of counterfeiting ensures or perhaps more accurately, *requires* a large margin of anonymity and therefore, us not sharing details was not taken by any offence to anyone who had asked. It was so that my life was extremely content until once day I made decision that changed my life entirely.

It was a bright day, as it seemed to always be. Esther was at school and it was early afternoon. It was just Charles and myself in the house working in the small office that had become our joint base of operations these passing years. And though the room was extremely cramped and not at all an inviting space to work in, due to the oppressive and almost unbearable heat in the summer – despite how many windows we opened and the similarly untenable freeze that penetrated through the room in the winter – I had come to revere the small office as a place that I could be close to Charles and enjoy the soothe that his companionship brought.

For the past week I had felt that my mind was consumed with thoughts of the man. He was the sole barrier between loneliness and the union that Esther and I could have made. I found him at once a person to venerate and to loathe.

I had not as of that point broached the courage to ask for Esther's hand a I was far too afraid of rejection, and so I quietly bid my time until I could work up the courage. The small snatched conversations and glances that Esther and I shared, told me that she thought I was also dragging my feet and I cold not bare to eventually see disdain and pity in those beautiful eyes. I had hope though that she still wished for me as every time I saw her, fleeting or otherwise, that stark blue ribbon shifted playfully in her artfully twisted braids. The presence of that ribbon gave me a continued hope everyday and so it was that that particular day I had found the courage to stop the careful copying of a one-hundred and twenty page will and call Charles' attention.

211

He was sat across from me at the desk, as the room was only big enough to fit one desk in it due to the copiously filled shelves that housed the various paraphernalia of our trade. He glanced up at me then, with his reading glasses perched delicately on his perfect nose, and though I was to ask something immense from him, in that moment I thoroughly hated him. Surely, a man such as he would wish for a suitor in similar stature to himself to marry his delicate sister, not a large brute such as I was?

Before I lost my composure however, I cleared my throat as best as I could and staring deeply into his brown and gold flecked eyes, lay out the inner feelings of my too-fast pounding heart. In the time it took me to finish my litany of half-pleading, half-bartering monologue of why I had to marry Esther, Charles had sat well back in his chair. His glasses now removed from his face and lay forgotten on the stained oak of our work desk. He had an unreadable expression etched thickly onto his usually so expressive and soft face. And I felt the heavy silence weigh down on me, as my body sat ridged, and the tightness within my stomach grew more profound. I could not anticipate his expression and imminent response.

For what felt likes hours though was only seconds. There was a long silence then. The room was usually silent when we worked – the nature of the job requiring a large amount of concentration. As any slip up could means hours of correcting to ensure no mistakes slipped through and brought down the whole business not just on us but our clients too. But in that moment it felt like the most tangible silence I had ever experienced.

After a moment Charles, who up until now had been blankly staring at me – or what felt more like straight through me – let out a defeated sigh. The type of sigh that wearied school teachers give to students who just wont take a lesson. He turned his eyes away from me and stood in the unhurried and languid way he always did, before telling me in no uncertain terms that for me to marry Esther was just impossible. Our relationship he said, was one of work, to involve Esther in it would be too confusing for her (despite her misguided ideas that she had relayed to me about wishing to marry me). He claimed she did not rightly know her own mind! And in a different more, sombre and sheepish tone, he admitted to having to keep a promise to his father's old acquaintance who had been promised, in a round about way by their father, to marry Esther when she became of age. This was the first I had heard of this and thought he was creating the story to put me off, until he took out a small key he used on a locked cabinet in the far corner that I knew held the house deeds and various other personal contracts. He rummaged around in the draw for the short time before pulling out a slightly browned set of papers which he fanned in the air for a moment before placing down in front of me. They were, he claimed as I unfolded them, a written contract of marriage from the gentleman signed by this allusive party, Charles' father and Charles himself. The document stated the acceptance of marriage between this man and Esther, with a grotesque and detailed itinerary of all that Esther, and by extension the family, would receive in their union. I did not need to have worked with Charles all those years to know that the article was

214

genuine and there was nothing I could do, short of killing the suitor, to make the horrific truth of the contract cease to prevail.

The sinking in my stomach only strengthened in its ferocity on seeing the contract and with shaking hands I placed it upon the table. I felt Charles' eyes on me – whether they were pitying or not, I was unsure and afraid to look up and find out. I felt sick. And truthfully, I knew my sick feeling was less about how Esther's freedom to choose had been taken away through this contract, that she herself seemed not to know about, but due to the injustice done to me. I had not met this suitor the whole time I had lived with them, surely I was a better choice than he to marry her? I may not have been as rich as he claimed he was in his vulgar contract, but I was as close to a member of their family as one could get! I lived in their house after all! The disrespect and blasé treatment towards me, turned my shock and sadness into righteous fury.

How could he deny me this? In fact how dare he deny me this? I kept this inner anger from showing. I may have expected a better outcome, but I was not a brute despite what he seemed to think of me, and I sighed just as he had. I placed my had over the crude contract that barred me from Esther and stood to withdraw from the room. I felt Charles' wary eyes on me the whole way out of the room.

The next few days passed as much the same as usual. I am ashamed to admit that I avoided esters eyes for sometime after the encounter in Charles' study. She sent me querying glances often and occasionally asked me if all was well. I ignored her for the most part, seeming to despise her as much as I did her brother; though I knew I could never truly hate her. The beautiful girl.

I was however, becoming much more hostile towards Charles, if he or Esther noticed they said nothing. The very presence of the man set my teeth on edge and though I worked well enough with him in the day and was civil for Esther's sake, the old feeling of him being in my way increased daily.

It was at this point, I am ashamed to admit that I began to engage in an unsavoury activity, or perhaps compulsion is a better word. I am not sure entirely what drew me to it, but I would often find that I could not sleep at night. The presence of Charles living and breathing in the room only a few doors down from mine, felt like an imposing presence in my mind. These thoughts prevented me from sleeping many nights and I lay awake numbly watching the lilting shadows on my bedroom ceiling.

I am not sure entirely what possessed me to do it, but one night I found myself getting out of my bed in the dead of night. I had no destination in mind, but I knew I needed to confront the oppression that was holding me down like a large weight upon my chest. I found that my feet took me to Charles' room that first night. I believe that I was perhaps in some kind of fugue state when my feet carried me there, as I seemed to have no control over my movements – like a passenger in my own body. I was not asleep and quite aware of my surroundings, but I could not stop myself moving.

Charles was apparently a heavy sleeper, for he never woke to any of the visits I made to his chamber. It was an odd sensation, not having the free will to move of my own accord but moving none the less. During these visits, I would simply enter his room that was cast in dark shadows, the curtains drawn-to every night, and stand just within the doorway watching him. I don't know what my subconscious was trying to achieve by this as I certainly felt no urge to do be there. I was a captive within myself, by my own unconscious mind to stare down at the man, the thing, that kept me from my one true desire, and simultaneously kept me in his house as a welcome guest and astute friend as though the entire heart-wrenching business in the office never occurred.

I stared down at him and I wish I could say that my mind was as blank as my body was, as it stood there. But when I had him in my sights, in that dim horrid lighting, I had the most violent and visceral thoughts of him. The thoughts were always much more dramatic and revolting than the last. A bloated body with blue and purpling bruises on the face, a deep laceration along the carotid artery another. I don't know where those came, indeed

218

sometimes they felt not at all like my own. But every night that my body woke me up to make its sombre and eerie way into Charles' room, I would stand motionless and think up the most horrendous ends to this man's life. Maybe he deserved those thoughts.

My nightly visits carried on for a good month, the whole time, Charles never awoke and had no idea of my visitations. I was still unable to control them, but his unawareness of me made it so that only I had the strange knowledge of what I was doing. I was hurting no one and so I felt no need to tell him.

A few days later, that was so similar to the day I had been so thoroughly rejected by Charles, I felt a deep feeling of déjà vu, Charles interrupted the quietude of the office. Without looking up from his notebook in which he was leisurely writing in his looping and rather effeminate cursive, he spoke in his soft voice. He asked me as though he was enquiring as to whether I had eaten lunch yet, whether there was anything I particularity needed in his room in the middle of the night. The question had me stop my attentive focus on reading an old house deed. I froze staring at Charles. With the guilt written so clearly on my face, you would not think I was successful at creating lies for a living.

Charles scoffed at the expression on my face, which quickly changed his handsome face into a mask of utter disgust. I cannot clearly relate what happened next in any profound detail, as I believe that my body was moving mostly on its own.

This uncovering of my nighttime ogling had Charles hurl the most distasteful and accusatory things at me, some of which I cringed at in their vulgarity. He accused me in no uncertain terms of preying on him as I could not have his sister. Which thoroughly denied because it was so far from the truth it was laughable, but he took my protestations as an admission of guilt.

By this point, I was immensely grateful that Esther was not home, as Charles' voice had raised a pitch and taken on an edge of pure seething hatred of me that I had never seen directed at anyone by this usually very calm man. He had moved to the door at this point and was gesticulating down the stairs. He wanted me to leave.

The home that I had created for the past five and half years with Charles and Esther was being destroyed. He had been awake at some point during my night wanderings and had not alerted me to his wakefulness, perhaps assuming I was there to do him harm.

I felt not so much ashamed in myself, as I could not help my movements, but I was embarrassed by Charles reaction. He was painting me as some perverse and vulgar creature that he couldn't bare to have in his house, despite the garbled and botched explanations that I tried to give him.

I swear, I only tried to get him to stop, I think I was crying maybe? The words hurt me so, I only wanted him to let me love Esther. I did not mean to hurt him, but he was so frail in comparison to my own bulk and I merely want to shove him out of my face, which he had reach into as he spat his accusatory vitriol. I shoved his bony shoulder and he stepped back with the force of it, but he was so close to the step and the soft smooth soles of his loafers slipped on the polished floor. Before I could reach out to grab him, his arm had flailed in front of me

221

as he tipped backwards, his head going straight down and his legs kicking up. I moved backwards to avoid getting kicked in the face. Pure instinct. He fell, the noise his body made as it thumped and bumped in different places down those hard, beautifully carved stairs was like nothing I had ever heard before. The noises stopped. I had watched him fall the entire time. I did not reach out for him. I suppose I could have, couldn't I?

I made my way quickly down the stairs, where his body lay twisted at the bottom. I could hear his raspy breathing and knew him to still be alive. I quickly reached where he lay in front of the front door to the house, and in a wide stretch over his prone body I reached over to the handle and clicked the lock to the right once – to lock the door from the inside. We had made quite a commotion after all.

He was still conscious when I came over to kneel beside him, he gurgled something to me though it was mostly unintelligible and I wasn't really listening. I looked around for a moment, searching. He wasn't dead – that needed to change.

He twitched his hand slightly in my direction and I let it drop back to the floor as I stood and made my way into the kitchen. The kitchen had what I needed. It was perfect in size, the sort of knife a street robber or inexperienced home robber would use. A small paring knife. I clutched it sturdily in my hand and made my way back over to Charles – his eyes looked unfocused as I peered into his beautifully shaped face. He had a cut high on his cheekbones, where I assume his glasses must have scratched him, as they fell off his face as he tumbled.

The next part, wasn't that dissimilar to what I had done in the past. I carved him delicately though, quickly – time would be crucial once he started screaming. Starting with his head, scream he did, but I ignored him and made haphazard slashes to the rest of his body to immediate the look of an unprovoked house break in as best as I could. I made sure to place a large deep gash in the shoulder that I had shoved, I was certain the area would bruise and become obvious once he was cold, and so I did my best to erase that small piece of damning evidence. I finished with a deep slash to his neck, which quieted him completely. He has nicely slashed when I had done, and I was fairly out of breathe, I had to make a few of the cuts in obvious places, and make the cuts shallow to bely the weight behind the stabbing. All to suggest a man less heavyset than myself.

I made speedy work of the house after that. I ransacked some of the more valuable items that belonged to Charles and Esther and hid them in a loose board under my bed that I placed my own intimate possessions, which were mainly old notebooks. Then I made sure to lock the door to our study and place the key in my pocket – our profession was still illegal after all.

Once I was satisfied with the state of the house, I quietly unlocked the front door and placed myself at the foot of the stairs; my legs draped artistically (I thought) over Charles' twisted and badly broken ankle. I clenched the knife, that I had placed on the floor beside Charles earlier, in my left hand and with a blank mind, plunged it straight into my upper right shoulder from behind, the angle was awful and I yelled out louder than I had intended to. The knife stuck just as I had planned at a lurid jagged angle in my muscle, that twitched as I breathed in shakily.

I slumped down with pain against the foot of the stairs and the wall, and waited for the pain and blood loss to drag me off into unconsciousness, as the wound bled horridly despite the plug of the knife sheathed in my flesh. I sat and waited for darkness and the return of my Esther, who would see this gruesome sight but would have no choice but to fall utterly in love with me all the more.

Chapter 8
Flood

Charles was dead. Everything planned out as I foreseen. Esther came home at some point and had raised help. I had fallen into a feverish coma for two days after the incident, and the poor girl was left to sort out the mess herself. I felt for her, but I fell even more in love with her after I saw how resolutely she handled her unexpected grief. She looked stunning in mourning colours.

I heard from the nurses that sweet Esther came to me in the hospital every day during my delirium, to sit beside me for hours until the poor girl was too tired to sit upright any more, and was put to bed the first night in the nurses quarters! What a delightful girl! Once my fever had passed I was able to assist Esther in sorting the arrangements for Charles' funeral – the good man had left her everything their father had left him in his will. In secret, I destroyed that hateful marriage contract. We were free to marry as we wished now and a week after the funeral I asked Esther if she would marry me. I initially feared that the proximity to her brother's awful murder by house intruders would put the skittish girl off the idea, but to my joy she jumped to the notion and a by the end of August we had married. I vowed to keep her safe from anything that may harm her in my vows – she did not know the full weight of those words. I believe I was the sole person in that church that did. Just as it should have been.

The take over of the business from Charles was not difficult, as many of the clients trusted me as well as they did Charles by then, and those that did not were inconsequential.

I noticed that my nightly wanderings had stopped since Charles' death. Now that there was nothing that settled on my consciousness, I suppose I was at peace within myself.

Esther though, became a constant in my life. She made me think only of her at all times. After a few months it

227

become clear that Esther had become pregnant. I was overjoyed with the news and I was so content with my life, that my actions that resulted in Charles' murder did not bother me. Although Esther was stricken with grief soon after Charles' funeral, the security of our marriage and the presence of a baby had improved her mood considerably. I was immensely pleased with this calm and satisfied Esther. She fit so perfectly into the world *I* had created for us – a beautiful space carved out by my disposing of Charles.

At night I would sometime slay awake. I was not suffering with insomnia as I had been before Charles' death, but something about the close presence of Esther, and the baby that was growing inside her, made me feel constantly on edge and alert. I would often lay awake staring into the lilting shadows of our bedroom as I listen the delicate and soft breaths leave Esther's mouth. On those nights I would lay there and I would inhale the darkness that surrounded us, and I would let myself drift. I would enter that space that is not sleep but not wakefulness either – an inescapable lucidity. During these moments I would feel as though my surroundings would all fall away until there was just shifting darkness and Esther's breathing. Her breathing! How I wished on nights to snuff out that breathing and leave just the darkness to encroach around me and swallow me whole!

••••

Ever since Charles I have been vigilant. Though the authorities made no suspicion towards me in regards to his death, I remained paranoid that my actions would catch up with me and I would be arrested.

So when I was pushed into my house by what felt like a rather large knife point in the middle of the day, I suspected that someone either a private contractor hired by a suspicious client of Charles', or a police hire was sent to get me to confess. The man was tallish, around the same height as me, dressed extremely well so as not to draw attention to the odd entry into the house. He looked like any usual caller that may grace our humble doorstep in the afternoon.

229

The man had large expressive eyes that for a wild moment, reminded me of Charles. He swiped my legs from underneath me and wrestled my arms behind me as he pinned me to the ground. I may have been large but I was no fighter, and this man clearly was. He placed the knife almost reverently against my neck, before I could choke out the confused outrage that was bubbling in my throat, the man began to speak.

He spoke in a lilting accent that I could not at all place. As he went on the incredulity in his reason for being there made me turn sour inside and I felt a distinct feeling of dread in my stomach. I wanted to shout for Esther but she was not home, and I did not want her involved in such a mess, better for her to find my body after the event. But to leave her alone? I couldn't.

Reckoning came when I least expected. It a rather ordinary looking man, and to this day I do not know who sent him; whether he was some friend of Charles' or of Joshua's – as the man claimed to be casting judgement on me for Joshua's death. I have to admit that the mention of my friend set me aback as I hadn't thought of him for years, but this man as he stood on my doorstep, a concealed knife in his jacket pocket, spat out how I had murdered Joshua.

It all happened so quickly that I had no real time to process more than that phrase. Esther was out shopping for food or some household goods, I have to admit that I wasn't really listening when she left. And so it was just me that afternoon in the house. It was quiet and I liked the house like that. It made me feel like I had my whole world under control, so when I answered the door, thinking it was going to be a client or some caller for Esther (as she often had friends from her school come and visit her) it is fair to say I was shocked to see that man stood there.

The man roughly pushed me down and I lost my footing and fell just short of catching my head on the bottom step. I was dazed and winded for a moment, but briefly and rather ironically I thought that this was the exact spot in which Charles had come to his end. The man did not wait for me to be acquainted with my surroundings, and preceded to kick the door shut and to press painfully onto my chest and stomach with his knee, the other foot planted firmly on the ground – his boot just inches from my head.

I made an effort to kick up into his back, but he was too strong. Although I was broad, I was no fighter and this man clearly was. He grimaced as I kicked him, but the mean look in his eyes threatened me to do it again. During that awful towards the floor, he had managed to grab both of my wrists in one hand and pin them above my head, catching the sharp point of the bone in my wrist against the wooden panelling of the edge of the steps. I cried out briefly but the closed front door made me doubt if anyone had seen it, and with the house being located not on the street-front but in the alley, made me doubt also that anyone would hear me yell out.

The man sneered down at me, his face was hard-lined and he appeared to be the sort of man that you would expect to be in company with Joshua. I was actually quite surprised that I did not recognise him myself, but I assumed that he was either an old friend of Joshua's before I come on the scene, or estranged. I had no time to think clearly on it however, because the man was bearing his weight down into my stomach, and stringing off a litany of fairly garbled insults and curses to me, despite him not knowing for sure if I had committed Joshua's murder. He seemed so certain in his righteous revenge, that he would not let me get a word in edgewise even when I tried to speak over him, his voice bellowed out and drowned out my own.

He had the knife pressed against my neck, though rather lightly as though he did not want to end my life in that very moment, but wished for me to listen to what he had to say first. It was then rather convenient for me, as when it seemed that the villain would make the decisive slice against my throat, with his sweating and labouring breath, in that moment the door opened and spilled into the gloom of the house, severe afternoon sunlight and Esther stood stock still in the doorway frozen most likely in fear.

The sound of the door opening and Esther's soft gasp and dropped bundles of groceries, had my assailant turn around – still pressing painfully on my legs and stomach, with the knife still pressed against my throat – though in a more haphazard fashion. He grimaced; I suppose not expecting for Esther to have returned in the middle of our intimate scene. He made to get up, I think he was going to force Esther to leave, but he did not move quickly enough. For Esther was going to be hurt, and the baby was going to be hurt – that was something I could not allow.

With a burst of strength, that I know not from where it of originated, I leapt at the man, grabbing his arm that held the knife and yanking it towards me. It did not really stop the strength behind him, but it did stall him in his movements and he turned his attention back to me and lashed out at me, catching the side of my face from my ear, down my jaw and towards my neck with the tip of the knife. The cut was deep but not fatal. I felt the pain but I kept moving forward and grabbed his wrist that held the knife. As he struggled with me to release the weapon from his hand, Esther by this time had shut the door behind her and shuffled further away from our commotion, her hands cradled protectively over her stomach. I wonder to this day why she did not run away to get help.

Our brief scuffle did not last long. The presence of two people perhaps, had unsettled my home invader and he seemed off guard. It was fairly easy therefore to catch him unawares. I tripped him using the back of his leg, and forced his considerable weight against him. He fell down with a heavy thud against the floor, and scrambled on all fours. I quickly lunged for the knife that had dropped rather conveniently right by my side, and in the blink of an eye I had stabbed the knife straight through the man's stomach. He let out a keening sound like a wounded animal – a sound I have never heard come from a human before. I stabbed him once more in stomach, once in the chest – aiming for his heart though I don't know if I hit it – and once rather grimly in the head. He stopped moving after that one. Esther was cowering, covering her face with one hand and protecting her stomach with the other. Her arm shading her eyes from the gruesome scene. She was covered head-to-toe in blood. Her white summer dress had been thoroughly soaked in it from collar to hem. And even the sleeve she was using to hide her face was now a pure crimson – I could not help but notice that that colour looked absolutely beautiful on her.

Covered entirely in blood that stuck to her dress and soaked and clumped together in the tangle of her braids – Esther seemed irreverent.

She had never looked more beautiful.

••••

235

The night was macabrely perfect for the discrete disposal. Esther was still severely traumatised from the events earlier, and she wished to stay home while I unburdened us of the body. I trusted that she would keep the secret. After all, the baby and I were all she had. The baby not being born yet, meant that she needed me, and my being arrested would not be beneficial to her.

I had taken the grisly business of dividing the body into smaller pieces in the shed that bordered the house. There was an old hacksaw in there and this I used to do the grisly business. I had decided that this would be an easier way to get the body out of the house, I had assumed and rather rightly, that nobody had seen the man walking to the house, and his disappearance would not be linked to me.   I will not go into detail about how the limbs were divided up. There was an old burlap sack in that shed, that was around the right size to fit the body in. I wrapped him a large bed sheet, that still leaked out of the cloth in large spreading red patches – but I would be leaving in the cover of night and I assumed that no one would see anything. The Lantern shone dimly in that shed that August night, as I sweated over the desecration of that man's body. A man whose name I did not even know. He was irrelevant. He had assaulted me and then accused me – this was the price that he was going to pay.

I checked in on Esther before I left, the sack of damning evidence in the yard, I did not want to leave it long for dogs or carrion feeders to find. And so checking in on my sleeping wife, I hastily scrawled note that I was nipping out to remove some bad food, hoping she would understand the message.

I walked rather briskly, my sack squashed close to my chest. Thankfully the canal was not far from the house, and I had left in the middle of the night at perhaps one o'clock – as I heard the steeple clock chime before I left out. I assumed, and rightly so, that there would be not too many witnesses about. I found a deserted area of the canal, with a sole bench with no occupant and a street lamp that had a thick layer of grime on it – the neglect of it, dimmed the light perfectly.

I wasted no time, and said no prayer as I dumped that large sack of meat into the river. The knife went along with it so no evidence need be left behind. I had thoroughly scrubbed the floors earlier and as I stood there watching the sack sink down, with the help of the large stones I had found on the riverside, I thought about how that floor in front of the step would never be the same – having the blood of three men, only one still alive being shed upon it. I knew that even though Esther was being very strong about what had happened, she could not stay that way for long. And I was correct, as a couple of days later, she was withdrawn and listless. I feared that she was not well enough for the baby, and I told her this. She promised she would get better and over the next few days a couple of her friends visited as they had not heard from her. They appeared to improve her mood considerably, and she was very good not letting on that anything untoward had happened. She told the that she merely felt ill and it was likely the pregnancy.

I worked less in those days, and Esther and I eventually decided that the best course of action for the two of us was to leave. I had heard from a client of mine that an island just off the north coast was fairly quiet, and he suggested that it might be the best thing for

Esther in her depressed condition. I wondered if sea travel was safe for her, and after consulting her doctor, found she would be fine, and that sea air might even improve her constitution. I proposed this to Esther tentatively, and she seemed to perk up at the idea of getting out of that house. Away from the house that had killed her mother, father and her brother. It was then hastily decided, and I quickly ended my work counterfeiting, which had become rather tiresome for me, and I thought of idyllic life that I could have on that island as a fisherman or some sort of marine job. I thought it might be good also for a child to grow up in the environment away from the sweaty, stinky, claustrophobic life in the city.

Grove island is what it was called, and when I asked the man why it was called that, and he simply shrugged his shoulders saying that perhaps there was a grove on the island. I found out as much as I could about it from passing ships, and there was indeed a grove island in the north. The climate was quite cold and extremely isolated, but the people on the island had very prosperous lives, with lots of fertile fishing grounds. It was reputed to be a very comfortable place to live, though I was of course advised to wait until Esther had given birth, by her lady friends, before travelling – as travelling with a baby would be a lot easier than as a pregnant woman. I pitched this to her several times, but she would hear none of it. The oppressiveness of the house seemed to grow on her day by day, and the bags under her eyes became more prominent and almost the same blue as the ribbon she still wore tied up in her plaited hair.

I made arrangements over the next few weeks, and we had booked a passage for the end of September. Over that time we had sold a majority of the things that still lay in the house, they were mostly her parents belongings, and we sold most of it at auction We received a comfortable sum for quite a lot of the antique furniture and paintings. Esther wished to take along the painting of her father, and as I did on the very last day of our stay in that house, wished to keep that photograph of her on her birthday when she was 17 years old.

I took it out of the frame tenderly and stared at that the picture for a moment. It was so well captured; the slight blue the ribbon in her hair was quite distinguished from the rest of her in the picture, even though it was in a black and white grain. I knew it was blue and that I that had given it to her – forever to be immortalised in that photograph. I folded it and placed it in my jacket pocket, wanting it close to me on our journey Esther at this point was six months pregnant, and I believed we were going to have a girl, Esther was steadfast in saying it would be a boy to commemorate her brother. I never verbally disputed her assumption, but I loathing the very idea of a reincarnation of Charles.

••••

The prospect of moving to an island that neither of us had visited before and had only known about through hearsay, excited me and I could tell that Esther was happy, though most likely not because we where going to that specific island, but more due to the fact that she would never have to step foot in that house again.

Whatever the reason, I was glad that she was happy and her health had come back – she no longer seemed wan and listless any longer.

The captain of the ship was a jolly man which was strange, for I had always known captains of harsh seas to be rather disagreeable. The crew also was a very kind, if not quiet and withdrawn. The other passengers made up an interesting contingent; besides ourselves there was a group of men that were heading to a large north-western island on some sort of scientific expedition, from what I could gather from their talk and the instruments that they had packed along with themselves, and never let out of their sight. There was also what appeared to be a journalist, or photo-journalist as he carried a large Canon with him, as well as another family including a father, mother, three little girls and a baby boy. Esther fawned over the baby boy as she truly believed that she carried one, I was still was certain that to was to be a girl.

Esther seemed to be reenergised on the water. When the weather was particularly dour, she enjoyed being up on the deck, and if she was not able to leave our small cabin because of a storm or tossing seas, she would grow restless and peer out of a small little porthole. I was therefore rather happy that we were going to live on an island that would be so close to the water, as she was so desperate to be close to it. I had never been particularly fond of the water, hence why I had never become a sailor myself and preferred to stay on land. Some of the men aboard often asked me what I did for work but I, for the most part, evaded their questions and if I did reply, I said that I was a bookbinder – as a lot of the work that Charles and I used to do did involve, to some extent, recreating entire books.

I cannot forget that day. It was the afternoon and the sky was dotted with a sparse collection of low-hanging clouds. It was early September and the sea was fairly still. I remember that day, the endless deep, had a shifting quality to it. It was blue, but in every shade and tone describable – aqua one moment and navy the next. I remember being mesmerised by it, and once or twice I thought the colour caught the exact shade of the ribbon that Esther still wore tied up into her braids.

Esther and I were stood on the deck and I was chatting to one of the scientists; Peter s*omething.* I forget his name exactly, it was *Peter James* or *Peter Jones* or something of that sort. He was a very average fellow, and couldn't help but remember that the suit he was wearing was a beautiful dark-brown tweed. Esther was stood silently besides me, not partaking in the conversation, but staring out into the water, as the ship pitching and rolled. By this time in the voyage, she had became an almost constant fixture on the deck of the ship. The sailors seemed to enjoy her company, and more importantly Esther seemed to be enjoying herself. I hoped that she was looking forward to Grove island as much as she enjoyed staying on the water. I remember the September day was unusually warm, but that sort of breeze that comes with beginning of water meant there was a cool wind and no humidity. Despite this, I could feel the sun beating down on the back of my neck, and I could feel the light and strength from it, but no radiating heat. I was glad, as summer was not my favourite season, and I was looking forward to having a child that would would be born in autumn just like his father.

The moment it happened is so unclear in my head. I remember almost everything I said to everybody that I spoke to, the birds as I saw and what I ate; but that one moment is so clouded in my mind it is as though someone had reached into my brain and simply painted over it. I had my back to Esther as I chatted to Peter James/John, when I heard a splash. Splashes happened all the time on the ship, the sailors would throw things overboard – occasionally dead rats that the cats would catch – that sort of thing. The sound of items being thrown over board was part of life onboard. That sound was admittedly louder but I thought not much of it and continued to talk to Peter James/John. It was only when I saw Peter's expression of confusion and then horror that I turned around to locate Esther and then slowly and rather embarrassingly, connected those two things in my mind – her lack of presence and the splash. Peter and I leant over the side of the ship. I shouted for help and soon everyone was crowded around.

How or why she had fallen I do not know, but I remember staring into the shifting tones of aqua, and seeing her face as it sunk further and further down into the never ending blue. I remember how the light rippled across her cheekbones, how the weightlessness of the water lifted her plaits around her head in ghostly tentacles. As she sank further down. Her face turned up towards the sky, she looked directly into my face. And what I saw was not the image of my wife, but that effeminate and languid face of Charles -it made me step back from the side of the ship. I don't know if it was disgust or fear, but I was briefly aware that Peter James/Johnson was taking off his jacket, that I so envied even in that moment, and dived in after Esther – doing what I should have done as her husband, but was too paralysed with shock, fear and confusion. I stared into the blue. I was most likely in shock, but I remember seeing passengers and sailors alike, running past me and leaning over the side. A woman I saw Esther speaking to often, but I did not know, gave out an ear piercing and, I thought, unnecessary scream when she had been told what had happened.

Two or three more sailors jumped into the water after Peter, but there was nothing for them to find. She was long gone, and Peter James/Johnson was brought back onto the deck, almost drowned himself – soaked with his lank hair plastered against his horribly pale skin. I couldn't help but think that the trousers of his tweed suit were are most likely ruined forever.

A sailor came up to me then, I recognised him as we had played cards one evening. He told me what I already knew from the Peter's face; that Esther was not to be found. For some reason in my shock, I only then noticed that my own clothes were actually quite soaked, I suppose the spray of Esther, and then three other bodies jumping into the water which had splashed back onto the deck in large quantities than I had realised in my state. My shirt and jacket were plastered to my skin, and my own hair was dripping droplets of water onto the deck – I was uncomfortable.

The sailor looked at me with remorse carved so deeply into his face, that it almost made me laugh – he did not know Esther! What grief could he possibly feel? Whereas I had lost my wife and unborn child. It was not my fault, but it felt like it in that moment. If had not frozen, if I had not turned my back on her, would she still be alive?

There was nothing that could be done and I retired to my cabin distraught and in shock. Many people, one of which was the captain came to knock on my door that night, wishing to pay their condolences to me, but I ignored the. For they did not know wife or unborn daughter- I was now entirely and completely alone.

The next day the captain held a funeral service for Esther. There was no body of cause to dispose of. I do not know why Esther did what she did. Did she not love me as I loved her? Did she see something in the fathomless deep that was more appealing that life with me? I don't know. All I know is that I no longer have her. The sea has claimed her. I was now to live my life alone again.

PART III – DEAD RECKONING

Chapter 9

Deep

The coffee pot fell from my hand.

It was almost comical, in its baseness. The heavy copper clanged loudly as it hit the stone floor.

It's burnished rim was deeply burnt through prolonged use, and now bloodied.

I stared for a moment, I couldn't not look at him as he lay there in the kitchen. His feet were pointing towards the rickety little table that we had sat at numerous mornings and evenings. His head had fallen at an odd angle.

He was dead.

He stared back at me – his large doleful eyes blankly looking up at me from the kitchen floor as his bandaged arm draped artfully across his torso. His head steadily stained the stone floor a deep beautiful crimson.

I had hit him and killed him, and I hadn't meant to.

Or had I?

I couldn't help but feel that some intrinsic part of me had intended to do what I did despite what my meagre conscious bleated in the contrary.

I had meant it.

If Ezekiel was no longer in the picture – and successfully disposed of as he was – then Sarah and I could live our lives together. The daughter I had lost could live *through* her.

That was what had happened, I had lost my little girl, unborn and she had been brought back to me by some divine intervention. I was not going to question it, and I had merely done what I had to do.

250

Sarah, was asleep in that unwelcoming and monotone sitting room. I had placed her in the wicker basket we often used to place groceries in. She was safe, I would make sure she was *always* safe, I would not leave her as I had my own child.

The slowly pooling blood around Ezekiel was growing larger and I stepped back, over the fallen pot, over the threshold of the door and into the narrow corridor that I had spent so many lonely days, before Ezekiel and Sarah, staring into. The whole time Ezekiel's gaze did not leave mine. For a dead man, I thought he was rather serene. He had no look of anger or fear even on his face, when I initially struck him. There was a brief look of shock and what was maybe disappointment that graced his lovely features before the expression died and his face became a lax mask of serenity.

I turned then, the hollow eyes burning into my back as I made my way to the sitting room. Sarah had not awoke. There had been little to no commotion really; the soft gasp that Ezekiel had made, the muffled thump of his body falling to the floor, on bended knees first, then the rest of him and the clang of the iron pot – which it it appeared was loud enough to awaken Sarah. Through it all, neither Ezekiel nor myself said anything. What he must have seen in my eyes before I hit him must have done all the talking.

I left the house quickly then, not stopping to lock the door and heading to my boat. I had not used it for months but I had kept it well maintained and it was waiting for us, bobbing easily on the dreary water. It was an old boat and gifted to me by a man who had moved on when I first arrived on the island.

I had never been given such a gift before.

The sky seemed brighter that afternoon. Though it was still predictably overcast it felt brighter, in fact that day it felt the brightest I had ever experienced on the island. The water through its same monotonous and vapid blue seemed to pulsate with subdued light. I felt at once rather queasy and clutched the basket that held Sarah tighter in my grip. She hadn't stirred at all, and slept with an almost corpse like stillness, and so clearly the swelling light was just my problem.

It felt as though I had never felt light like that before in my entire life. My body seemed to be engorged on this new feeling. I was gradually becoming light-headed and was compelled to place Sarah down on the ground for a moment as I regained my senses. I cast my gaze back to the house that was roughly around ten paces behind me. The door still stood ajar, thought I noticed that in spite of the open doorway the light from outside seemed to not penetrate into the hallway at all. The light was swallowed up by the gloom of the house and I couldn't help but feel that it was rather fitting for the loneliness that that house embodied. I had been alone in a house that stood apart, I had lost everything, but now I was retaking a little of what I had lost in Sarah. It was my due.

I turned again, away from the house this time and turned my gaze back to Sarah who was peacefully sleeping in her basket, and not stirring at all. It was as I did so that the ground seemed to swim dramatically underneath my feet, and the brightness of the day searing into my eyes. I pitched forward into the sand as the sparkles remained behind my closed eyes. The brightest day I had ever witness anywhere, was impressed in my mind.

••••

The soft swaying, is what awoke me, I think.

I was accustomed to how being on water felt though I couldn't really say why. I had not really been on that many boats or ships other than my own once a month or so. The confusion then, is perhaps what truly pulled me out of the deep void that my mind had retreated to.

I remembered the brightness just before I had fallen. Sarah. Was she okay? Where was she? My concern for her is what forced me to open my eyes. I was immediately forced to close them again. The luminous tendrils of sunlight that shimmered all around me was so piercing that I couldn't see properly. I was on a boat somewhere and the *sun* was shinning. I could actually feel the heat of the sun! I hadn't seen the sun properly since I had moved to the island. The majesty of it after not seeing it for years was particularly striking, and it took me a few moments of blinking erratically (and I was still squinting through my eyelashes) before I could keep my eyes open. The tears that leaked out the corners of my eyes were a small price to pay too actually experience sunlight fully. The next thing that I noticed was the vast deep-blue that surrounded me on all sides – I had been correct in my initial thinking that I was on a boat. The gentle swaying was the motion of my body as it was propped upright against the side of a small dinghy.

I knew a few of the islanders owned these sorts of boats, but I did not. The fishing boat that I intended for Sarah and I to leave in was by no means this small, simply pieced together little boat. There were no extra fixtures or even paddles I noticed. I immediately noticed also, that I was not alone in the boat.

As I squinted in the harsh sunlight and tracked my gaze across the boat, the lack of Sarah and the presence of someone else became markedly apparent. Although I was aware of the state that I left Ezekiel for some unexplainable reason, I was not surprised to see him. For moment, I looked at him in pure shock. I had no idea where we were and he seemed untroubled – the wound that should have been obvious at his head was not there. And the scar from the wound he should have had from his first arrival on the island was also missing from his naked forearms.

My sluggish mind noticed somewhat belatedly that he was wearing the same clothes that he had on when he arrived on the island, but they were in perfect condition as though they were brand new. His left eye however, was still blind and seemed fathomless and luminous in that golden sunlight. His face appeared diaphanous in that light and though there was no expression his face, I felt it was directing pity and distaste towards me. This made me sit up against the side of the boat where I was slouched in a gross contrast to Ezekiel, who was sat upright and proper. His shapely hands lay lax and gently clasped in his lap as he stared back at me.

My shock soon turned into anger though, but I struggled to speak. My mouth felt as though I hadn't opened it in years, it felt coarse as though it was full of salt water residue.

"Sarah is fine," Ezekiel quietly provided, while he cast his gaze away from me to look out into the endless blue. "She was never really here, but that's not the point. Not yet. She's fine." He added as though a reassurance; "if you wanted to know".

"What do you mean? Where is she?" Not that I forgotten about Sarah, but Ezekiel bringing her up made me further concerned.

"That isn't necessary for you to know just yet," he emphasised, though in a way that I thought was rather facetious. He angered me. The poise with which he sat there as though he had done nothing wrong! But he had! He had taken my child from me, I knew it! I was to take his in exchange, that was only fair.

"You knew her did not you?" I did not need to say it explicitly, I know he would understand what I was referring to. I couldn't help but ask it! He was to show up in too similar circumstances as he how I lost Esther.

"I did not," as he replied in that languid voice of his as his eyes turned from the horizon and to the water. He stretched his slender arm into the cool blue that looked *so* inviting and waved his hand around for a moment before retreating with something that looked like shredded fabric that was covered in salt-crust in his hand. "But even if I was to explain that you couldn't understand." He paused as if in thought, "Even if you wanted to. Not yet."

"You keep saying 'not yet'. Why not now?!" Finally, the shock of waking up where I was, besides Ezekiel seemed to wear off. I was angry. "How is it you're here? I don't understand, I hit you! And quiet fatally too! I saw you bleeding! There's no blood anywhere! How did we get out *here* Ezekiel?"

The mention of his name seemed to bring his full attention back to me. I noticed that his dull eye was brighter than ever, as though it had its own source of light. Even his skin I thought seem luminous in the sunlight, as though he was radiating his own daylight. It concerned me, how little time I had spent in true sunlight, for me to be afraid of Ezekiel simply sat in it.

"You don't understand where you are do you? You haven't figured it out yet?" The questions were asked to me in the tone that one would soothe a child. It irked me to to no end, but before I could interrupt Ezekiel continued – the piece of salty, green-blue tatters still in his hand. "I did not take Esther in the way that you believe. I did not take her at all, but I was definitely sent here to you. Don't you think that much?" After a pause he answered for me. "Of course you do, you think there is a connection between your wife and I."

"There is!" I couldn't help yelling. The emotion was too raw, though it was only the two of us out there on that eerie water. Once the admission was out of my mouth, I couldn't help but feel rather embarrassed. Ezekiel had not stopped looking at me, and his face had not changed during my outburst. Instead, it was I that had to look down and away from him, ashamed and feeling those eyes; one dead and one alive, peering calmly and serenely at me.

I doubt, I would have noticed it had I not looked down, and I had felt nothing prior. But as I looked down into my lap, I could not help but notice what I hadn't before; that my clothes were torn and shredded as though I had been wearing them for years and years, and had walked thousands of miles in them. The seams were frayed and the stitching had rotted in place, there were cakes of dust maybe and what looked like silt or mud in the creases of my trousers and shirt. My vest had lost all the buttons and lay open over my once white shirt that was now a dirty brown-grey. I knew the clothes to be mine, though I had never seen nor worn them in this condition.

It was the same suit that I had worn a year ago when I came to this island. I had often worn the various articles of it at different times throughout the year and had never known it to be in this shape. There were thick stones or what could have been barnacles clustered in the folds of my trousers, and where I had turned up the cuffs of my shirt. I was not afraid but fascinated. It was not as though these things were just now appearing, but as thought they had always been there and I could only now see them. The seaweed that was wrapped around my limbs, like artfully designed jewellery, shimmered wetly along my body in the sunlight and contrasted so drastically with my washed out skin. The usual deep brown of my skin was now broken up with a mirage of colours; blue and green bruises fanned out all across my exposed skin. It was miraculous, and the more I stared at it the calmer I became. I felt as though the tension that was held inside me was being slowly drained out. I looked up to Ezekiel but he was gone. Leaving no trace he had been there at all if not for the piece of tattered salty, blue fabric he had clenched in his fist that lay in the space he had just inhabited. It was clean now though, and a startling deep blue. It was velvet. A thin and delicate soft piece of blue velvet. I stared at that blue and reached for it.

Now in the water. Nothing had changed, I had not blinked, the boat not "disappeared" exactly, but now it was not there and I was afloat. My clothes now wet through. I could not feel it though, as my body was cold. It felt as though it had been this way for a while. The ribbon I had let go of, and had floated out of reach. I watched it for a moment and understood.

Floating on my back was easier – it let me look at the sky that was so blue and beautiful. The sun bore down on me with kindness, and I felt aware. The water lapped around my body in playful waves, that buffeted me side-to-side softly, and slowly encroached further and further across my body until only my face was exposed to that august sun. The rest of me was unfeeling. I felt so far down in the water that was so blue but so opaque – a dazzling kind of darkness that was impenetrable but still so intense. Not quite yet the inky blackness that was far below, but patiently waiting.

It covered my face now, and I understood.

-The End-

Afterword

Thank you for getting to the end! If you haven't read the entire book and you're here, that's not how books work! I'm really glad you got to end with me! This was a really fun book to write! It was a long process though, and there were times when I wasn't sure that I wanted to even continue writing it! I am very glad that I did though and I hope you enjoyed it as much as I had writing it (not so much editing it all!)

The character development of Josiah especially was really difficult. I was trying to get his broken personality to appear repressed at the beginning and in *Anchor* you realise he's a bit of bastard. I hope that came across clearly.

And now, ladies and gentlemen and everyone in between, the moment you've all been waiting for... the explanation!

The Island

So Grove Island is pretty weird right? There's a reason for that, its actually Limbo, or Purgatory or whatever you want to call it. If you did not pick it up in *Dead Reckoning* Josiah has been dead for the entire book. He drowned with Esther at sea on the way to perhaps an island that looks exactly like Grove.

The islanders as you may have guessed if you're a very astute reader, are slowly passing over. When they no longer exist or can be found on the island and appear to get brighter as in the case of the Doctor and his wife, they are making their way to either heaven or hell,

In particular I enjoyed writing Grove island as being so strange. The low light at night time I took off the real nighttime phenomenon in places like Iceland which I think is so cool and would love to see in real-life one day

The clouds in particular I thought was fun addition to the island – the days all being the same overcast and sunless scape was intended to mimic the idea of monotony of limbo.

As to why I chose an island and the nautical theme, I suppose it's a personal interest in the sort of coastal/sea area and the closeness, I think, to danger and death. I knew I wanted Josiah to die at sea when I planned out the story, but I wasn't sure when or how to do it at first; the idea of making him live in a sort limbo state was interesting to me and I can't say rightly where the idea came from but I'm gad it blossomed as well as it did!

The metaphor

The whole book is a metaphor for retribution and judgement... in a sense.

Everything that happens in Anchor is Josiah's actual life- that is what he is being judged on in *Dead Reckoning*.

I feel like the plot here is solid but there's always room for extra interpretation and I think that's what makes books engaging. Basically, the book is intended for the reader to get two different perspectives of Josiah and judge his life from the small snippets you get from is monologue.

Is Josiah justified in how he sees the world and the people he interacts with?

Or is he spoilt and undeserving? *I'm* not telling you the answer.

Josiah

I don't want to go into too much detail here, because I would prefer everyone to come to their own conclusions about him. The point in Josiah character development is to show how he thinks the world is against him and how he thinks he is owed something.

The beginning of the book and the way that Josiah interacts with Ezekiel is supposed to suggest that he is a nice person when really he isn't. After all, he's looking after a man and child that need his help with seemingly no want of compensation.. that's good right? Or maybe he's doing it to make himself feel like a good person because of the bad things he's done in the past?

Ezekiel

I'll leave a question that has no definite answer here: *Is he supposed to be an angel?*

Sarah

I think people might miss out the significance of Sarah in this book and focus on Ezekiel as his name is in the title, but I think Sarah is so important. She is more of an anchor to Josiah than Ezekiel is after all. She is the key piece that connects Josiah to the life he lived, and its more that Ezekiel is the vessel that connects Josiah and Sarah together.

Josiah and Ezekiel

I know for certain that people will say that Josiah is in love with Ezekiel or at least superimposes the idea of his wife in the place of him, but I would say that's only partially true and not close to being how Josiah truly sees Ezekiel.

Ezekiel I think, is more seen by Josiah as something or somebody to covet. He has the seemingly whole life that was taken from him, as Josiah would believe in an unjust manner, he sees the loss of his wife and daughter as something that can be replaced in Sarah and Ezekiel.

But I think that to Josiah there is no romantic or emotional love towards Ezekiel, he sees him as a means of proving to himself, that he is a good person. To paint himself as not the man whose questionable actions we see in *Anchor* drive him.

One of the things I asked myself and my poor Instagram followers when writing this, is whether or not Josiah a psychopath. I suppose its hard for me to say that he is as I'm not a psychologist, but maybe a joint English literature and psychology major with be able to analyse his behaviour and let me know.

Printed in Great Britain
by Amazon